COACH QUINN

from the creator of...

The *Of Music and Men* novella series and the *Of Music and Men* podcast series, available wherever you get your podcasts.

A STORY BY KAYONA EBONY BROWN

"EPISODE ONE – THE CHALLENGE: FLAG"

SIINGLE LIT
Washington, DC
2025

Coach Quinn by Kayona Ebony Brown

SIINGLE LIT
Published by the Siingle Group, Ltd.
Siingle Group (USA) Ltd.,
600 Pennsylvania Avenue SE #15530,
Washington, DC 20003 U.S.A.

First published in 2025 by Siingle Lit., a division of Siingle Group (USA) Ltd.

ISBN 978-0-9786725-3-9 (print)
ISBN 978-0-9786725-2-2 (ebook)

Publisher's Note
This is a work of fiction. Unless otherwise indicated, all the names, characters, businesses, places, events and incidents in this book are either the product of the author's imagination or used in a fictitious manner. While this novel draws inspiration from real individuals, events, and brands, all characters, names, and situations have been fictionalized or altered to protect privacy. Any resemblance to actual persons, living or dead, is purely coincidental.

www.siinglegroup.com

United States of America

CONTENTS

ACKNOWLEDGMENTS

A few years ago, I connected with two brilliant journalists, Lyndsey D'Arcangelo and Frankie De La Cretaz. They had just written a book together that was set to come out later that year called, *Hail Mary: The Rise and Fall of the National Women's Football League* (NWFL). Now, I've been a football fanatic my entire life, but I had never once heard about this all-women's tackle football league that *almost* took the country by storm in the 1970s.

Hail Mary has had a major impact on my life and career. After devouring the book within days, I became obsessed with the stories of women risking every aspect of their lives—motherhood, careers, marriages, and their societal images as "women"—for $25 a week playing football. Back then, what a woman did or didn't do was under a significant microscope, and small minds believed women had no business in football.

The stories that centered this league and its women were endless. *We Are the Troopers*, by author and historian Stephen Guinan, who has become a good friend of mine, tells the story of the winningest team in pro football history, the Toledo Troopers. *The Herricanes*, a documentary by Olivia Kuan, whose mother was one of these women who played in the NWFL, is also excellent. I even got the chance to add to this catalog myself when I produced a short feature for the NFL on the GOAT of women's football, Linda Jefferson.

Women *love* football. In fact, we made up about half the fanbase even before our beloved, Taylor Swift, made her impression. So, while developing this story, I couldn't help but have Sam Rapoport top of mind. Sam is a literal "game changer." Among many things, she is responsible for women being more than just fans, but actually having a pathway to NFL jobs, including coaching! So, you can probably understand why she was a motivating factor for this story, especially the main character, Quinn.

Although this tale is a work of fiction, it is also a proverbial "tip of the cap" to all of the female-identifying folks who have helped move the game forward—from those of the NWFL way back in the 70s to the no-longer-hidden figures working to advance the game in the greatest American sports league today: the National Football League.

Now, it's not so surprising to see women as owners, team and league executives, on the sidelines as interns and assistants, or even out on the field as refs. But as of the 2024-25 season, we have yet to see a woman advance to the position of coordinator on either side of the ball, which means we could still be years out from seeing a woman running a team as its head coach.

But that didn't stop me from imagining it!

After a conversation with another female football lover, this story was conceived. It is a tale created to not only entertain but also inspire a new generation of women to continue shaping the game we all love.

In American football, situations will arise that a team may want to challenge. Head coaches have what's called a "challenge flag" in their pocket, which is a red cloth that's weighted on one end so they can toss it out onto the field to signal that they want to dispute a call—to investigate the veracity of what was determined in the heat of the moment by the officials.

Throwing a challenge flag is another way of saying, "Are you sure 'bout that? Look at it again, but this time slow it down, zoom in, maybe pause it, rewind it, look at it from another angle, and then another angle, and then do all of that again a few more times to make sure you see what you thought you saw."

In the National Football League, the referees will go to what's called, "the replay booth," a designated little video hut on the side of the field, to review the call of the last play. Here, they can access multiple camera angles and consult with replay officials, but the final decision is often made in conjunction with the "Art McNally GameDay Central" in New York, the league's central replay review hub designed to ensure consistency and accuracy across all games.

Now, there are a few rules that go along with using this tool, like the types of plays and calls that are considered "challengeable," how many challenges a team can have in a game, when they can actually be used, and when they *don't* have to be used to get a play reviewed with the hopes of having a call overturned. To the naked eye, it can seem quite... chaotic.

But putting all of the logistics and the rules within the rule aside, the challenge flag, at its core, is basically a way of seeing things differently, more clearly, and more precisely—for better or for worse.

THE NIGHT MEETING

The urban landscape in the near distance across the Harbor was a scene from inside a souvenir snow globe that was just activated by a forceful shake. Only, Charm City didn't seem to boast its usual magnificence and touristy excitement. It was blanketed by a hue of gray and dusted by aimless precipitation that brought with it an eerily muted, almost deafening silence.

And yet, there was Quinn—right in the middle of it all.

She wandered in what felt like an endless circle— trekking on a determined mission to get to… Well, she didn't actually know where, as the wind howled across Federal Hill Park, sending flurries swirling in every direction, refusing to fall as snowflakes should. Instead, it was alive, dancing violently all around her like tiny, icy daggers. But even the cutting chill that came with the wind seemed distant, with its harsh whirling like a whisper in Quinn's ears.

Wearing just a tee shirt and blue jeans, Quinn's overly exposed deep brown skin had no choice but to accept these conditions, so she hugged her arms tightly as she trod through the snow. Her coat was missing, maybe left behind in some rush she barely remembered. The cold crept into her bones, but she didn't flinch. The pain was temporary. Movement was necessary. Each step she took left a print in the thin dusting of snow, but even that was whisked away almost immediately as if her presence had never been there at all.

She wasn't headed anywhere in particular. Not consciously, at least. Her mind was elsewhere, swirling through memories like the snow around her—a jumble of thoughts she'd rather forget but couldn't help replaying. The mistakes, the successes, the what-ifs…

And then, she saw something.

A hat—no, a fedora—lying ahead on the ground, half-buried in the snow. She squinted through the storm, her curiosity piqued. There was something about it, something out of place in this modern setting. The wind took another violent turn, and the fedora lifted gently from the ground, gliding toward her as if summoned.

Quinn stopped, bent down, and scooped it up. It was heavier than she expected, stiff from the cold, yet soft. Her breath became snagged in her throat as she caught sight of a man ahead, standing with his back to her. Tall, although not towering, and his frame sturdy enough to support him in the bitter cold. He seemed out of place too—his clothes, his demeanor... like something pulled from a different time period.

Slowly, Quinn approached, naturally assuming the fedora must have been his. The snow crunched beneath her shoes as she neared him.

"Sir... your hat..." Her voice, usually firm and confident, sounded weak against the wind. He didn't hear her. Maybe he couldn't, or maybe he didn't care. She kept approaching, drawn closer.

"Sir?" Quinn called again, louder this time, holding the fedora out like an offering.

The man finally turned.

The smile he wore was soft, perhaps even angelic, but something about it sent a chill down her spine far colder than the gale or the frosty flakes ever could. Recognition flashed across her eyes. She knew him! She was sure of it. But how?

And then... the scene began to slowly change form, like ice to water to invisible vapors as it evaporated into a cloud of nothingness, gone from her presence without a trace, like it had never even happened.

"Fourth down. Curious to see what the Cards are gonna do here..."

ACT ONE
THE CONVERSION

The iconic voice of legendary announcer, Jim Nantz, introduced this division battle—his smooth, conversational tone held its steady cadence with descriptive, yet detailed thoughts, despite the gravity of the high stakes.

The roar from the Santa Clara landmark was deafening. Levi's Stadium was alive with the sound of 70,000 rabid fans echoing through the stands, their voices blending into one continuous hum of anticipation. No one sat in their seats, all eyes were glued to the battle unfolding on the field below.

The crowd's collective breath hung in the air as the Cardinals' offensive coordinator, Quinn Canals, watched from the sidelines, headset on, her face set in steely concentration.

As her hazelnut skin glowed under the Bay Area afternoon sun with an intensity that reflected the fire burning beneath her calm exterior, her signature silk press shoulder-length hair lay tucked tightly beneath her headset. She examined the field with savant-like precision, chewing her gum with a steady rhythm, her face an impassive mask of focus, unfazed by this relentless pressure. With just 34 years lived and only a half foot over five feet, she was a tower of stoic determination—her lean, athletic build was a testament to her years of discipline and dedication, living the lifestyle that football demanded. She was a study in calm—a leader with a job to do.

The scoreboard read 42-41 in favor of the 9ers, with the Cardinals down to their last play. The clock ticked down to 22 seconds in the 4th quarter. This was it—4th down on the 49ers' 41-yard line.

The tension in the air was palpable, thick enough to cut through. Quinn's heart pounded much slower than the shouts of the crowd, and outwardly, she was as still as an oak tree—a breathing technique she used as another instrument of control. Her mind was a machine, processing possibilities, calculating risks, and planning for any outcome. The entire game rested on this next play. And this was her moment.

Watching this on TV, you heard Nantz as he continued to break down this nailbiter: "Instead of the long field goal attempt, Cards OC, Canals, is opting to go for it."

"Yeah, this is a gutsy call," added Tony Romo, the former Cowboy-turned-commentator, whose raspy, energetic voice brushed color into every syllable of analysis. "But remember, her kicker missed his last two attempts from this distance, so she sees this as four-down territory. A missed field goal and the game's over. She's playing to win."

On the field, the QB stood in shotgun formation, the center ready to snap the ball. The 49ers defense, poised and ready, brought the blitz.

"Blitz coming. Pressure on. He tosses it to Lynch, who's wide open! And he walks into the endzone! Touchdown Cardinals!" Nantz's voice rose with the excitement of the moment.

From the sidelines, Quinn's unflappable countenance didn't change as her offense celebrated. She knew better than to celebrate early—there were still 14 seconds left on the clock.

"I tell you what, that's just great coaching right there by the offensive coordinator, Quinn Canals," Romo said, praising her play call. "She saw that blitz coming."

Boos from the crowd filled the stadium as the Cardinals' running back taunted them, celebrating his walk-in touchdown. On the jumbotron, the replay unfolded in slow motion.

"That's called a 'scat protection,'" Romo explained. "Such a clever play-call by Canals where she says to her running back, 'If that linebacker comes, don't block him because he's also the guy that would have to cover you in man-coverage.' Brilliantly done. Executed perfectly."

Nantz added, "She has orchestrated one of the

most creative offenses this season."

"Top five in everything, easily putting up 48 today against a good defense," Romo explained. "But when they're giving up 33 a game on the other side of the ball, no doubt her offense isn't the reason why this team has only won eight games all year."

Quinn exuded an air of quiet confidence, something undeniably focused about her—a sharpness in her eyes and a precise, calculated way she moved. Her face was unreadable—stoic, rarely giving away what she was thinking. She had mastered the art of keeping her emotions in check, knowing full well that as a woman coach in the male-dominated world of professional football, she would be given no room for anything less than perfection... which was what she had just delivered in what would be her final play call of the season.

Quinn, still focused on the field, quickly signaled to the team to stay on and go for two.

Marty O'Callaghan, the Cardinals' intense, hard-nosed, 67-year-old head coach, whose face was beet red in the moment, came sprinting toward her down the sideline, waving the team in off the field while ushering the special teams out to kick the extra point.

Jim Nantz's voice clarified the confusion. "Canals wanted to go for two. I think O'Callaghan just overruled her."

Quinn calmly held her arm out, stopping the

kicker from heading out onto the field. She covered her mouth with her play sheet to covertly discuss her reasoning with O'Callaghan, knowing she was being watched by cameras and eyes around the stadium. But when her shoulders slumped, it was clear—she'd lost the argument. She dropped her arm and the kicker jogged onto the field.

"You know what? I would trust my OC in this situation. If she feels that confident, I believe she had something special dialed up," Romo said, noticing Quinn masking her frustration. "O'Callaghan might be making a mistake."

Quinn and O'Callaghan continued their discussion on the sideline, but they couldn't be heard in the broadcast. Nantz and Romo proceeded with commentary, assuming what the discussion could've been about.

"O'Callaghan just wants to get the easy points here," Nantz explained. "If they got the two-point conversion, the 49ers would have to match it to tie. But on the off chance the 9ers score a touchdown, all they would have to do is kick the extra point to win."

Romo chimed in: "Yeah, the extra point doesn't make real sense here for Arizona. The 9ers still have time to do something. Canals' thought was to prevent San Fran from beating them with a go-ahead field goal, and I get it, but the 9ers' QB has been lighting this Cardinals' defense up. I know it's just 14 seconds, but they might've left too much time on the clock.

Either way, the 9ers need a touchdown to stay in it."

On the field, the extra point went through the uprights, putting Quinn's Cardinals up 48-42. O'Callaghan walked over to Quinn, confident in his decision, and leaned over. "See? 14 seconds left. All we gotta do is hold 'em for 14 more seconds."

Quinn remained stone-faced, not bothering to respond. She knew how long 14 seconds were.

The kickoff sent the ball soaring into the end zone. It looked like the 49ers return man would take a knee and settle for the 25-yard line, but then...

"Jim, I think he's bringing it out!" Romo shouted.

The 49ers' return man went straight up the middle. The 5, the 10, the 20... Uh-oh.

Jim Nantz's voice rose in surprise. "Smith goes up the middle! They can't bring him down! He's got one man to beat!"

His blocking was superb, and after he broke his first tackle and slipped by two more, the only one left to beat was the kicker.

The return man, Smith, cut past the kicker, leaving him stumbling. The fans were exploding as the 49ers returner raced down the field.

"It's a footrace! He's going to go all the way! You can kiss him goodbye! 101 yards for the touchdown!" Nantz shouted, the stadium exploding in cheers.

Quinn stared out at the field, her anger concealed in a sedated glare, while letting her clipboard drop to the ground with a thud. She finally looked over at O'Callaghan, but he refused to meet her eyes. The clock showed 0:00, and with the extra point, the 49ers won the game 49-48.

Romo's voice came in once more. "You can't help but think: had they gone for two like Canals wanted, maybe we'd be in overtime right now, and maybe the Cardinals could've been able to spoil the 49ers' playoff hopes and end the season on a high note with a win."

Quinn, along with the rest of the Cards coaches and players, converged on the field to congratulate the 9ers and shake hands in a show of sportsmanship.

As the 49ers celebrated, Nantz added, "Instead, San Fran gets a wildcard spot, and Arizona drops their ninth of the season. Good news is: they hold the number five pick in the draft–"

"Do you think O'Callaghan and this staff will be making that draft pick?" Romo asked more directly. "I mean, third straight losing season. I don't know. But you gotta feel for Canals right now. She led this offense from dead last four seasons ago before she arrived to one of the top-ranked offenses the last two years–"

"And let's not forget the obvious," Nantz added: "first ever female playcaller in the league. McVay, Shanahan, Reid—Canals could be up there soon."

Romo agreed, "She's just as clever, just as tactical. And this is just the beginning. Mark my words, she'll get some serious consideration for head jobs this off-season."

As they spoke about her in detail for the broadcast audience, the camera followed her as she shook hands and spoke for a moment with the head coach of the 9ers about something that couldn't be heard by anyone else.

"She's gotten looks before," Nantz reminded without going into the story about how she lost out on the Buccaneers' job last season to a famous coach who decided to come out of retirement. "There've been questions about her ability to lead men and her readiness to helm a franchise—"

"All due respect, that's silly," Romo said, clearly taking offense. "For any owner or GM to think that way is just flat-out crazy. She's proven she's among the brightest play designers in the league right now. She has the experience. She has the training. It's time."

As Quinn turned and exited the field for the last time as the Arizona Cardinals' offensive coordinator, Romo's voice continued as the bed of the broadcast.

"I believe we're looking at the next great NFL head coach, who will just so happen to be the first-ever female head coach in NFL history."

The sound of the stadium faded as Quinn disappeared into the darkness of the tunnel, her future uncertain but her resolve unshaken.

THE RAIDERS

The news came down like a hammer. BLACK MONDAY had struck—the annual NFL tradition of firing coaches right after the season's final regular-season game that Sunday.

As expected, the Cardinals cleaned house. Marty O'Callaghan was out. The general manager, gone. The entire coaching staff was now out on the street. The headlines splashed across every sports outlet, from ESPN to local Arizona stations: "CARDINALS FIRE HEAD COACH O'CALLAGHAN, SEEK FRESH START AFTER DISAPPOINTING SEASON."

Everyone knew it was coming—O'Callaghan's third straight losing season had all but guaranteed it. But there was something about seeing it in print and across social media, seeing her own name mixed into the swirl of speculation and judgment, that felt... hollow. The league was always looking for a story, a new headline, something to grab attention.

Her name had become that story:

Cardinals' OC Quinn Canals in New Orleans for First Head Coaching Interview

Canals in Charlotte as PANTHERS Eye Offensive Genius for HC Job

Former Cards clever OC heads to TITANS, HC talks

NY JETS call Canals to talk open HC job

Could CHICAGO be a good fit for Canals, offensive genius?

"It's Super Bowl week, and the hottest name on the head coaching market is former Cardinals offensive coordinator, Quinn Canals." Colin Cowherd's enthusiasm was bursting through the speakers. "Canals, the offensive savant who led one of the top passing and running offenses, not to mention one of the most creative minds on that side of the ball, is in Vegas today to interview for their head coaching vacancy, so we're gonna talk about whether we think it's a good fit because 'fit' is everything…"

It was hard for her to block it out. Between social media and traditional media, she couldn't open her phone or turn on the TV without hearing her name. If she read newspapers, she would've seen herself there too. She clicked out of the app and chose to ride the rest of the way from the airport to the facility in silence.

Anyone else might have been nervous or excited; Quinn maintained a sense of calm. Sure, she wanted this job, perhaps even more than the others, but she knew better than to get her hopes up. She wished she could skip this part and go right to signing her deal, standing next to whatever team owner at the press conference, and talking to us about how she was going to take the team from losing to winning. But she couldn't skip this. This was part of the process.

Her entire life, it seemed, had led up to this moment. Ever since she was a kid, all she'd wanted was to be a head coach in the National Football League—a six-year-old girl on career day at school describing to her class and the teacher how she wanted to draw up plays for her home team, the Baltimore Ravens, and lead them to a Super Bowl.

Of course, she got laughed at because… Well, that wasn't a thing. Girls didn't coach NFL teams. She was crazy. Her teacher even asked her, gently, "What about something else? A backup plan." And to that, she responded, "Well, I would accept the Cleveland Browns job. I'm sure it'll be open."

But today at 34, preparing to go on her fifth interview in three weeks, Quinn was feeling something else. This was what she had been waiting for—what she had worked for her entire life. This was a feeling she just didn't have the vocabulary to articulate.

The media loved to tout her accomplishments with flattering headlines: *First female play-caller in league history. Architect of one of the most creative offenses in the NFL. Poised to be the NFL's first female head coach.*

But what the articles inside actually talked about were the "quiet parts"—the things no one dared to say out loud, but what they all were thinking. It was an unspoken doubt of owners and executives, a constant question that hovered in the air like a cloud that followed her:

Is she ready to lead an NFL team?

The midday Vegas sun glared off the sleek black-and-silver facade standing like a fortress in the desert—Raiders Headquarters, a monument to power and success. The dry heat was relentless, but Quinn barely noticed as she stepped out of the black SUV that had driven her there. Her focus was sharp, her nerves tightly contained, just as they always were before a big play. This wasn't just another interview; this was her shot at the future she'd been chasing all her life. The Raiders—a cornerstone franchise, one of the most progressive organizations in the history of the league. This just felt right.

But Quinn had attended enough of these things to know the drill by now—the meet-and-greet, the tour of the facilities, the subtle dance of proving yourself without coming across too desperate… This was her fifth visit in the last three weeks. Fifth time's the charm, was a saying she was hoping to make "a thing."

A warm gust moved her hair from its preferred position; her silk-press style and shoulder-length cut had become her signature look—always impeccably neat, a sharp contrast to the chaos around her. It was part of her persona: polished, put together, and always in control. And she was never one for flashy accessories, preferring a practical, clean look that reflected her no-nonsense approach to both football and life. On the sidelines, it was always J.Crew khakis, white Chucks, and a team-branded top, but today, it was a business suit: black with pinstripes and a silver shirt—the Raiders' colors.

Waiting at the entrance was Mark Davis, the Raiders' owner, unmistakable with his bowl-cut hair, white fanny pack strapped around his waist, and a cup of iced tea in hand. Mark was the son of the late great Al Davis, a pro football legend and the original Oakland Raiders' owner since its founding in 1960, who was known beyond the field for his activism in civil rights. Quinn held a great admiration for Al.

As she approached, still in awe of the building behind him, Davis smiled wide, his posture casual but his eyes keen and assessing. Beside him stood President Morgan, a sharp, power-exuding Black woman, a former attorney with an aura of authority, and GM Kent, an upbeat former athlete who carried himself with an easy confidence. Their presence told Quinn everything she needed to know—this wasn't just another formality. They were taking her seriously.

Davis extended his hand. "Ms. Canals, welcome to the Las Vegas Raiders. Glad you could make it."

"Thank you, Mr. Davis," Quinn replied, her tone even, though inside, she could feel the familiar tingle of anticipation.

Inside the building, the cool air was a welcome contrast to the desert heat. The headquarters was just as polished and modern as she'd expected, its decor all silver and black complimented with white, reflecting the cutting-edge brand of the team, the raider—a pirate-type figure with an eyepatch, leather helmet, and two swords behind his head with a bold sans-serif font—which greeted her on the floor as soon as she stepped in.

They led her to a large conference room, its windows offering an impressive view of the training facilities. The table was set, and Quinn took her place across from Davis, Morgan, and Kent. She placed her folder of plays and notes neatly in front of her and took a deep breath; this was the moment she'd been preparing for.

Davis leaned back in his chair, iced tea still in hand, and smiled. And then, he broke the ice…

Now, Quinn heard this opening question that had been laid out for her, and in fact, she should've been expecting it because it was the same icebreaker she'd heard in every interview she'd ever had in her life. Instead though, because nerves had surprisingly showed up now, her mind snapped into the mode she knew best: "Yak took on two split wide, 66 hitch on Vegas flare. On one, yak it yak it with the 124 thump shallow Mamba X pylon eight six. Or my secret sauce, which is near left H2 chip double drag goes half-back balloon dummy spot call hard three. I like to call that one 'Barbie and Ken.' But my favorite… is 12 Victory."

Proud of herself, she almost smiled at that last part, feeling a brief flicker of satisfaction at the clarity and precision of her delivery as she added: "That's a knee. That means game."

The room was silent. You know how they say, you could hear a pen drop? Well, an ink pen actually did fall from the table and hit the floor, and it was noticeably loud. That's how quiet it was in the room.

Davis, who had been nodding politely at first, now looked confused. He raised his eyebrows, glancing at Morgan, who offered a small, tight-lipped smile in return. Then he turned back to Quinn, his brow furrowed.

"The statement was… tell us a little bit about yourself," Davis said, his voice a bit slower, as if trying to guide her gently back on track.

Quinn blinked, not realizing her mistake. She'd gone straight into play-calling mode, talking football when they wanted something else. Something more personal. But what could be more personal than football? She had poured everything she was into the game.

She straightened slightly in her chair, trying to adjust. "Well, sir, that was about everything you need to know right there."

Davis chuckled awkwardly, but there was a hint of discomfort in his eyes. He shifted in his seat, then glanced at Morgan and Kent, clearly unsure how to respond to her answer.

President Morgan, a poised, formidable woman who didn't miss a beat, jumped in to steer the conversation in the desired direction. "What he meant was: you're originally from Baltimore, where you've been coaching football since you were in middle school; you studied Mechanical Engineering at Dartmouth, where you got a rare football coaching scholarship, and graduated with honors." She gave Quinn a pointed look as if to remind her that there was more to being a head coach than just calling plays. "You start your day at 4AM, you have dinner at 4PM, you study Nietzsche, you like Spike Lee movies... And your coaching idol is Andy Reid who helped you when you first got into the league. You came up through the Women's Forum, worked as an intern and assistant for six clubs before landing the coordinator position with Arizona three years ago— first woman ever to do so—where you turned them around and led perhaps the most creative offense in the league this year."

Quinn's eyes flicked between them, her expression tightening. She didn't care about the biography, about the details of herself that had been laid out a thousand times in interviews, articles, and scouting reports. What mattered was the work. The winning. She kept her face neutral, but the irritation simmered beneath the surface.

"You could've saved us all the time and filled him in on all that before we started," Quinn replied, her voice sharp, though her face remained composed.

An uncomfortable silence followed. Davis fidgeted slightly, glancing again at Morgan as if unsure how to proceed. The dynamic had shifted, and not in Quinn's favor.

After a beat, GM Kent leaned in, attempting to salvage the moment with a more personal question. "So what would you say is the best way to connect with your players?"

Quinn's answer came immediately. "Winning." Her voice was firm and decisive. For her, there was no other answer.

The room fell into another tense silence. Davis shifted in his seat, rubbing the back of his neck as if trying to find the right way to respond. He smiled, though it didn't quite reach his eyes.

"You're... terse. Yeah?" Davis asked, his voice casual but probing, trying to get a better read on her. Everyone at the table smiled, sensing the awkwardness, but Quinn didn't join in.

"I speak at length about things that matter, sir. Football matters. Where I went to school? Not so much."

Her words hung in the air, the tension thickening. Davis seemed unsure how to respond to that. He stood abruptly, signaling that the interview was over, or at least that he had gotten what he needed from it.

"Well. It was a pleasure meeting you, Ms. Canals. Your reputation… certainly precedes you." Davis reached out to shake her hand, his smile tighter now, less certain. Quinn stood, matching his gesture, but she could feel the disconnect. Something had gone wrong.

As Davis left the room, GM Kent followed, leaving Quinn with President Morgan, who lingered behind for a moment. Morgan regarded Quinn carefully, her expression thoughtful.

"Try to… open up a bit next time," Morgan advised, her tone softer, though still sharp. "You have amazing football instincts. But socially? Maybe try doing the opposite."

Quinn narrowed her eyes slightly, not quite sure how to respond. How does one try to open up? She wasn't here to be liked. She was here to win.

Morgan paused at the doorway, turning back with one final comment. "You want this job badly, yeah?"

Quinn nodded, though the irritation still simmered beneath the surface. "Yes."

"Then… just exhale."

And with that, Morgan left, the door closing softly behind her, leaving Quinn alone in the polished conference room, her thoughts spinning. She had just been through what was supposed to be one of the most important meetings of her career, yet she felt... lost. She clenched her fists at her sides, frustration gnawing at her. Football was what mattered. Winning was what mattered. And yet, somehow, they always wanted something more.

And with this came... the waiting game.

Before she could gather her things, the same short, white woman who had brought her water before the meeting started, stepped in and waited by the door, presumably to show Quinn out.

"Is there a restroom around here?" Quinn asked.

The woman barely looked up, pointing absently, "Down the hall and to the right."

Quinn took her things and left the room to go in that direction. As she proceeded down the hall, her pace slowed as she focused on the large TV mounted on the wall ahead of her. The screen was broadcasting a sports show, and a familiar face flashed across it: MJ Acosta-Ruiz, breaking news in her usual high-energy delivery.

The banner at the bottom of the screen read: *BREAKING NEWS: LAS VEGAS RAIDERS HIRE BEN EUBANKS AS HEAD COACH.*

Quinn stopped dead in her tracks.

She stared at the screen, unable to move, her

body frozen as if the world had suddenly come to a grinding halt. Ben Eubanks? The Packers' offensive coordinator?

The realization hit her like a punch to the gut.

It was over. They'd already made their choice... before she even stepped foot outside the building!

She wondered whether her interview had been nothing more than a formality—an obligatory nod to the media buzz surrounding her name—or if it was something else.

She felt the weight of the place pressing in around her, the walls closing in. The air felt suffocating. Her chest tightened, her pulse quickening. All the hours she'd spent preparing, all the late nights perfecting her schemes, her vision, her strategy... and for what?

Her eyes remained locked on the screen as Acosta-Ruiz continued to talk, but the words blurred into the background. The reality was... it was over.

THE DRINK

The Super Bowl was just hours away, and the Dave & Buster's was packed—a noisy, crowded sports bar with arcade games, flashing lights, and TVs broadcasting Super Bowl coverage. The air buzzed with pre-game excitement and the constant hum of people enjoying their drinks and food.

At a table in the back corner sat Mike, the Cardinals' former offensive line coach—a good-natured Teddy Bear of a guy, mid-40s (think older Jason Kelce). He'd told Quinn to meet him for drinks, but what he hadn't mentioned was that others from the Cardinals' former coaching staff would be there, too: Dean, the animated and intense, tall, lean wide receivers coach in his late 30s, with Sarah, the super-fit, lover of laughing and debating, newly 40 strength and conditioning coach, and Johnny, the assistant running backs coach, the most reserved among this group of elders, and the youngest at just 30.

Mike sighed, sitting up in his chair. "That movie sucked. Plus, they sold me on it being a true story. It wasn't even a true story. The guy was duped."

Dean shook his head, defending the film. "It won awards!"

Mike rolled his eyes. "It was Sandra Bullock! I bet *we* could come up with something for Sandra fucking Bullock and it'd get awards."

Sarah smirked, taking a sip of her drink. "She is amazing. She can literally do no wrong."

Johnny chimed in, his tone serious. "Seriously. She's incredible."

Dean waved his hand, dismissing the argument. "Okay, fine. Greatest sports TV limited series of all time?"

Johnny leaned forward, immediately answering, "Easy. *Queen's Gambit*."

Sarah raised an eyebrow. "*The Queen's Gambit*? That's not a sports show!"

Johnny was undeterred. "Yes it is! Chess is a sport. Anya Taylor-Joy transformed into an elite fucking athlete, and you know it!"

They all began to talk over him, laughing and dismissing the claim. Mike, still laughing, patted Johnny on the back. "He's got a point. The brain is a muscle, right?"

Sarah quickly stopped laughing. "Aw, who invited Buzzkill Lightyear?"

Across the room, they spotted Quinn entering

the bar with a messenger bag on her arm. She didn't notice the group immediately, so she looked around, uncertain about how much time she would spend in this place. She wasn't here for drinks or games, but Mike had invited her, and after everything that had happened, maybe a distraction wasn't the worst idea.

Sarah rolled her eyes. "How much you wanna bet that's homework in that bag."

The group shared a knowing laugh, but Mike stood up to go greet her, his expression softening as he saw her standing across the room. "Guys, seriously, be nice. I invited her—figured she could use a friend or two, given... everything."

Dean leaned back in his chair, crossing his arms. "Heard she didn't even make it out of the Raiders' building before they announced Eubanks as head coach. Ouch."

Sarah winced. "Oof. Very fucking ouch."

Dean shrugged, his tone more casual now. "And the way things are going, it looks like New York, Atlanta, Tennessee, and Carolina are filled, too."

Johnny leaned forward, his voice quieter but still pointed. "It's not going to happen for her this year. And with all those interviews..."

Sarah, unable to resist a jab, said facetiously, "Gee, I wonder what it could be..."

Mike waved a hand at them, shaking his head. "Come on, cut it out. She's here. Be cool."

Quinn stood at the entrance, scanning the

room. She almost turned and left. This wasn't her scene. She didn't do "fun" or "relaxation"—not when her mind was still buzzing with unfinished plays and strategies. But Mike had been so insistent.

"Quinn!" Mike's voice boomed from across the room as he raised his beer so she could see him approaching to meet her halfway.

"Aye! I didn't think you'd actually come," Mike said, his tone warm as he met her.

Quinn looked over in the direction he came from and noticed the group across the room at the table before answering. "You didn't tell me everyone else was going to be here."

Mike grinned sheepishly. "The big game is just an excuse for us to be in Vegas. Come on, sit down, have a few."

A Cardinals fan—a gruff dude in his 30s, wearing a Fitzgerald jersey—brushed past them. His gaze hardened as he spotted Quinn, his expression filled with the kind of disdain that accompanies the smell of a foul odor.

"You should've gone for two. No wonder nobody wants to hire you. You're fucking pathetic," the fan muttered, his voice dripping with contempt as he recalled her last game against the 49ers.

Mike stepped in immediately, his expression darkening. "Hey, buddy, keep it moving, alright?"

Quinn sighed, her face giving nothing away, though the words stung. She didn't respond.

Mike gave her a gentle nudge. "Listen, we couldn't drink to anything all year with all the losing. This could be your chance to finally connect with these guys and talk about something other than out-scheming a 4-3 defense with an Air Raid attack."

Starting to open her bag, she said, "Oh, I actually have some new thoughts on that. You basically just have to—"

"I don't care," Mike cut her off, waving a hand dismissively. "It's Super Bowl Sunday, for fuck's sake. Relax!"

At the table, Sarah, Dean, and Johnny continued their conversation about Quinn, attempting to squeeze in some more gossip and personal opinions before she got to the table.

"The thing is, she doesn't have a life, so the rest of us couldn't either," Sarah muttered, glancing at Dean.

Dean nodded, leaning forward to add: "If you arrive on time, you're late. If you go home on time, you're not 'committed.' Oh, and a simple conversation with her made me feel like I was in fucking special ed."

Sarah arched an eyebrow, teasing him. "Don't like smart women, Dean?"

Dean raised his hands in defense. "Hey, I'm not saying that—"

"Players seem to be okay with her," chimed Johnny, who had been mostly quiet until now, finally adding two cents.

Dean shook his head, leaning back in his chair. "Nah, respect and fear are two different things. Players are just scared they'll lose their spot if they don't follow her crazy rules."

Sarah added pointedly, "She tried to bench the number two draft pick. The owner did not like that."

Johnny nodded, but his voice remained measured. "In her defense, the backup was a much better fit for her system."

Sarah shot Johnny a look. "Whose goddamn side are you on, Johnny?"

Just then, Mike and Quinn arrived at the table, Mike's arm still around her shoulders. His voice was loud and jovial as he announced her arrival.

"Look who agreed to drink with us!" he exclaimed, giving Quinn a gentle push toward the table.

Quinn forced a smile, but her discomfort was clear as the others greeted her with half-hearted enthusiasm. As the waiter approached with a tray of drinks, Mike turned to him with a grin.

"Bring her one of your strongest–"

"Oh, no, I don't drink alcohol," Quinn said, shaking her head.

Sarah mumbled under her breath, just loud enough for Quinn to hear. "Maybe you should."

Johnny, always ready with a suggestion, piped up. "Get the Island Punch! It's like mostly pineapple juice. But also entirely rum."

Quinn's voice remained steady, though her words were blunt. "Alcohol contains ethanol and other chemicals that have considerable toxic effects on the digestive and cardiovascular systems, and act on the brain and body in a similar way to carcinogens. Since alcohol is a drug, it can cause unwanted symptoms, poisoning, even death by asphyxiation."

Her words silenced the entire table, and for a moment, even the bar seemed to pause as everyone turned to look at her.

The waiter stared at her, wide-eyed, unsure how to respond. "So... is that a 'no' on the rum or...?"

Mike turned to Quinn, his voice low and a bit more serious now. "Canals, look around. This is a place to relax and have fun with friends."

Quinn didn't flinch. "You are not my friends," she said, her voice cold. "You're co-workers. *Former* co-workers, in fact, which, despite the time together, doesn't qualify automatically as friendships."

Mike sighed, his shoulders dropping slightly as he tried to reason with her. "Listen, it's been four weeks since any of us have done the thing we love the most. Today is the final game of the season and then... who the fuck knows? None of us are where we want to be right now. This is our last and maybe only chance to do something together as a coaching staff."

He softened his tone, giving her a warm smile. "I promise you, one drink for first-time sake will go a long way in making a connection here. And for the record, kid: I don't care what you say, you're my friend."

Quinn accepted this without an argument. And then she looked around the table, at the expectant faces watching her. She sighed, knowing she wasn't going to win this one.

Finally, she nodded and looked at the waiter: "One Island Punch."

The table erupted in cheers as if they had just won something worth celebrating after a long season–

FLASH!

Quinn. Mugshot. Side profile. Blank stare. Glossy eyes. Shame, embarrassment, fear…

FLASH!

Quinn. Mugshot. Front-facing. Same blank stare. A prisoner only of her own thoughts, knowing that the future just became that much more uncertain.

ACT TWO

THE STARLINGS

B ack at her apartment, Quinn stared out the floor-to-ceiling window. The Arizona landscape spread out before her, brown and blue hues blending into each other like a perfect impressionist painting. She barely noticed it as she turned and dropped down, draping herself across the sofa, allowing her mind to become distant and disconnected.

The TV droned in the background, its familiar cadence of sports talk filling the silence of the room. On the screen, Josina Anderson was discussing the latest moves in the NFL, but her words barely registered in Quinn's mind.

"This is shocking because I've spoken with several people in the Cardinals organization, and no one was aware of any issues like this with Canals," Anderson said, her voice cutting through the haze. *"As far as they knew, she was a girl scout. Now, with the Super Bowl behind us and February coming to a close, we head*

into the offseason with Chicago being the only team left with a head coaching opening. And since they haven't already brought her in for an interview, I think it's safe to say this incident puts Quinn Canals' last remaining coaching option in serious doubt."

The words landed heavily in the room, though Quinn barely reacted. Her face was flat, her emotions locked away. Only the slightest glimmer of moisture appeared at the corners of her eyes, but she blinked it away, unwilling to let herself feel anything.

She relaxed back on the sofa with a deep breath, falling victim to the comfort of the world behind her eyelids, while willing the noise of the TV to fade as she tried to push the thoughts from her mind...

In this world, Quinn was back on that cold, windy, lonely street in Baltimore. The snow whipped around her, biting at her skin, but she continued walking, her steps steady. Up ahead, she spotted something on the ground—a fedora. She bent down and picked it up, feeling the weight of the hat in her hand.

Looking up, she saw a man in the distance, his back turned to her. She recognized him, though she couldn't place how. She continued walking toward him, the fedora held tightly in her grasp.

Everything around her suddenly froze. The snow stopped falling. The wind stopped blowing. Even the flag overhead paused in mid-wave. The world had gone silent, the air thick with confusion.

And then, the man turned toward her. His face glowed with an angelic light, a soft smile dancing on his lips. Quinn's eyes widened with recognition...

And that's how it went sometimes when she fell asleep. Seven more weeks went by and at least one night in each of those weeks, she found herself wandering the cold, windy, snowy street in Baltimore, always almost getting the chance to give that mysterious man back his fedora.

But this time—this random Tuesday night now in the middle of April—a voice, seeming to be coming from the sky, echoed throughout this atmosphere:

"Now, as the league gets ready for the draft in two weeks, eight teams will go in with brand new head coaches..."

She looked up and around, confused by this broadcast that didn't fit the time/space reality of where she was—standing on a street in Baltimore. But she'd failed to realize that she was, in fact, in a dream. However, before that could compute, the iPhone "Opening" ringtone zapped her from her fedora mission back to her apartment in Phoenix.

With her body still draped across the couch, she reluctantly allowed her eyes to peel open. The TV was still playing ESPN in the background, giving details about nothing that even mattered much anymore.

"And in breaking news, Alana Ari, the Olympic sprinter from Maryland, failed to place at the season opener Miramar Invitational by a tenth of a second. Ari

once sought to be the first Jewish woman to win gold in the 100-meter track and field event for the American team, but her recent struggles on the track puts that goal in doubt..."

Quinn barely heard the broadcast. As the phone continued to ring, she leaned over and picked it up, looking at the screen for a quick moment before accepting the FaceTime call.

"Yeah?" Quinn's voice was low, emotionless.

Mindy Tanaka's glowing face appeared on the screen, her agent.

Mindy was an almost 50, deal-making, optimist with a bright, borderline bubbly personality that contrasted sharply with Quinn's more serious demeanor. She was always energetic, approaching every challenge with a level of enthusiasm that often felt unrealistic. But to her credit, as Quinn's agent, Mindy was resourceful and relentless, using her charm and connections to push for opportunities, even when the odds seemed slim. Despite the high-pressure world she worked in, Mindy remained upbeat, often trying to soften hard truths with brightside positivity. Beneath her friendliness, though, was a savvy businesswoman who knew how to navigate the tough sports landscape while keeping her clients' best interests in mind.

"Quinn! Hey, how's my favorite coach?" Mindy greeted, her tone full of energy.

Quinn let out a light, humorless chuckle.

"Coaches coach, and right now, I'm just on the couch. I guess I'm couching."

Mindy laughed, not missing a beat. "Well, how do you feel about Baltimore?"

Quinn's eyes sharpened at that thought. Baltimore? Her hometown? She hadn't heard anything about the Ravens being in the market for a head coach, but if they were? She quickly sat up, her interest piqued.

"It was fine the first 18 years of my life," Quinn said, her forehead relaxing as she allowed herself a glimmer of hope. "I suppose coaching there won't hurt. Why? What did they say?"

Mindy's smile widened. "Baltimore wants you, baby!"

Quinn's heart skipped a beat. Could this really be happening? She tried to keep her excitement in check, but it was hard not to imagine the possibility of coaching for her hometown team.

But then, a flicker of doubt crossed her mind. "Baltimore has a coach. And an OC–"

Mindy's expression faltered slightly, her tone shifting as she prepared to drop the catch. "Okay, so... it's not *exactly* the Baltimore Ravens."

Quinn's face fell. The pause that followed was long and heavy with anticipation. Mindy hesitated, then finally spoke.

"It's... it's the Baltimore Starlings."

Quinn blinked, confused. "The what?"

Mindy sighed, clearly searching for the right words. "It's a bird. A *fierce* bird. And it also happens to be… a football team. Flag… football."

The silence that followed was deafening. Quinn could feel the disappointment creeping in, but Mindy wasn't done.

"In a growing flag league," Mindy added quickly, trying to put a positive spin on it. "But it is professional, so…"

Quinn's patience snapped. She hit the red button on her phone, ending the call abruptly. The phone dropped to her lap as she leaned back against the couch, closing her eyes again.

Flag football? Seriously?

The phone rang again. Quinn let it ring a few times before reluctantly picking it up.

Mindy's voice was urgent now, almost pleading. "Listen, Quinn, they *really* want you. They want to fly you out tomorrow. The owner is the Under Armour guy. He's putting you up at the Four Seasons, the whole nine. The NFL is behind this flag thing hard, and I think… I think you should give them a listen."

Quinn shook her head, her voice filled with disbelief. "Is this all you can come up with—flag football, Mindy? Seriously? What have you been doing the last two months while I've been—"

Mindy cut her off, her tone firm but compassionate: "NFL, NCAA Division I, II, and III, hell, even the UFL. None of them were calling, so I started calling them..."

Mindy hesitated, then continued, her voice softening. "But Quinn... the reason you haven't gotten another job is... it's not because of the Dave & Buster's thing, although that's obviously not helping."

Quinn's breath was caught in her throat. She wasn't sure she wanted to hear what was coming next, but she had to know. "Tell me. I'm a big girl. I wanna know."

Mindy's voice was quieter now, almost reluctant. "Well... you have a Tom Coughlin problem."

Quinn frowned. "What does that mean?"

Mindy sighed. "You're Tom Coughlin. But not everyone has the Giants' patience."

The words hung in the air, and Quinn felt the weight of them settling in. She understood now. It wasn't her talent, her knowledge, or her strategies that were holding her back...

It was her.

And if you don't know, Tom Coughlin was the head coach of the NY Giants back in 2004, who was known for his strict discipline, old-school mentality, and hard-nosed approach. Players hated this dude. He didn't know how to connect with people, he was too inflexible, and to top it all off, he wasn't winning.

So in 2006, the Giants considered firing him but instead, the owner came to him and suggested he take a different approach with his players. He did a startling personality makeover, turned things around, and ended up leading the team to two Super Bowls in his time there.

But those early years were infamous, and the truth was that most teams didn't have that kind of patience—not then, and certainly not today. If no one likes you and you're not connecting with people—and on top of that, you're not winning—you're gone. Or in this case, your reputation precedes you, and you're not hired in the first place.

Mindy's voice broke the silence again, softer now. "Quinn, people hire people they like. And... the truth is? People... don't... like... you."

The truth hit hard, like a punch to the gut. The hum of the TV filled the uncomfortable silence, but Quinn couldn't hear it anymore. All she could hear were Mindy's words, echoing in her mind.

People don't like you.

This wasn't new. Quinn was brilliant—no doubt about that. Her mind was a finely tuned machine, capable of breaking down the most complex defensive schemes in a matter of seconds. She didn't just understand football; she was a master of it. She saw patterns and designs where others just saw chaos. Her mechanical engineering degree, earned with honors, had proven her ability to think both analytically and exactingly. Everything in her life, from the plays she drew up to the way she moved through the world, was based on logic and efficiency.

But brilliance, for all its rewards, had a cost.

Quinn's intelligence was her greatest asset, but it was also the source of her deepest flaws. The same precision that allowed her to see a linebacker's movement before the snap also made her impatient with anything that didn't serve an obvious and specific purpose. This was where her intelligence became a double-edged sword.

She could see patterns and predict plays and even players, but she couldn't always predict people. Her bluntness and arrogance made it difficult for her to build the personal relationships that were so critical in her profession. Her co-workers respected her genius but kept their distance socially. Players followed her, but they didn't gravitate toward her casually.

In situations like the one at the Raiders' headquarters, she dove headfirst into what she knew best, believing that it was the most important thing— the only thing that mattered. But that's not what people wanted from her. They wanted a connection. They wanted someone who could smile, share a funny story, build rapport. Quinn had little patience for that. In her mind, the scoreboard was the only thing that mattered. Who cared if they liked you, as long as you won? People like winners. So as long as she was winning, she figured, the people would eventually warm up to her.

But when Mindy, her agent and ally, had said it plainly: "People don't like you," the words stung, not because they were cruel, but because they were somehow still true. Still, in her mid-30s, the feeling she'd felt her entire life—the words she'd heard for the first time from a schoolmate when she was 6— were still true. She had outgrown a lot of things, but to know that after everything, she hadn't outgrown that... was a pain she couldn't believe she was still enduring after all these years.

For Quinn, life was football. But to the rest of the world, life was something entirely different, and they navigated it with a set of rules to which Quinn hadn't learned the playbook—and it included doing the things that made you "liked."

And so she looked down at her phone, exhaled, and once again forced herself to try and play by their rules.

* * *

The flight had been smooth, but the weight of her thoughts had made it feel much bumpier than it was. Baltimore—her hometown. She hadn't been back in almost a year. She hadn't expected to be back like this.

As she rode in the back of the black Escalade they had sent to escort her from the airport to the headquarters, she saw everything through a different lens. The landmarks were the same—the stadiums, the Harbor, the familiar grid of streets she had played on as a kid. But everything else just felt... different.

She didn't feel like she was coming home as a success story. She wasn't returning as the first female head coach in NFL history like she had once dreamed. Instead, she was coming back as an unemployed failure, here for a job she didn't even want, in a league she hadn't even heard of, with people she didn't even know..

The street leading up to the Starlings' headquarters was different from the rest of the city she passed to get there. This felt serious and industrial like it was an area specifically set aside for business and business people. There were no single-family homes and no pedestrians, only buildings converted into yuppy lofts with no drywall and exposed HVAC stuff—more "cool" than it was cozy.

She noticed the colorful van double parked up ahead of them as her ride stopped, but she hadn't yet noticed the guy tussling with the blonde pit bull near it on the sidewalk until her driver hesitated to get out so he could open the door for her.

"Woah," the driver said, deciding to stay and watch from the safety of the SUV. "Let's let him figure this out first."

He was referring to Noah, the guy who was probably regretting having signed up to take on animal rescues. He was a clean-cut, brown-skinned brother who looked more than fit enough to handle the frisky hound he was losing to.

Quinn decided to open her own door and step

out of the ride, unfazed by what was going on with the animal. She happened to love dogs and was really good with them, but that was a story for another time and not one she was going to share right then with the driver.

"Come on, Swifty. That's it, girl," Noah coaxed, holding onto her leash as she tugged against him.

Noah barely noticed Quinn or anyone else around as he struggled to wrangle Swifty, the playful pit bull he'd been trying to load into the back of the animal rescue van. Swifty, full of energy, darted around the sidewalk, making it nearly impossible for Noah to get her inside.

With one final burst of energy, Swifty dodged the van door, slipping out of Noah's grasp, and was off down the street.

"No, no, no!" Noah shouted, chasing after her. His sneakers slapped against the pavement as he ran, weaving between parked cars and light polls, trying to keep his breath.

Swifty's tail wagged furiously as she dashed past a sleek, modern building engraved with the name "STARLINGS" in bold letters. Noah barely noticed the building as he ran past, focused solely on catching the runaway dog.

Just like the exterior, inside the Baltimore Starlings Headquarters, the building was impressive— polished, modern, the kind of place built to make you feel like you were part of something big. But despite the sophisticated decor, Quinn felt a sense of detachment. No matter how legitimate the facility looked, this wasn't the NFL. And she knew it.

Greta McFly was waiting in the lobby with a bright smile and a double-clutching handshake—more than happy to meet Quinn, she was clearly honored. Greta led Quinn through the facility on a tour; she moved with the kind of confidence that could only come from years of being in control. At 52, she was tall, slim, and impeccably dressed in a tailored pantsuit that gave her a sharp, no-nonsense edge and an innate sense of authority. Her short, platinum-blonde hair was slicked back, highlighting her angular face and striking cheekbones. Greta carried herself with a quiet authority, the type that commanded respect without needing to demand it. She had an air of efficiency, like someone who wasn't used to hearing the word "no."

Greta's voice was polished and professional as she continued the tour. "We have the best facilities in the sport to accommodate our athletes. Plus, our partnership with the Ravens provides marketing opportunities no other organization has."

As they walked, Quinn's eyes scanned the space around them. The Starlings' logo—a stylized purple and gold bird—was displayed on the walls, the team's colors threaded through the entire facility. Everything looked legitimate. Competitive, even. But Quinn was unmoved, still processing the fact that she was here in the first place.

Greta led them to a small sitting area, where the chairs matched the team's logo and colors—purple, black, and gold. They sat down, and Greta smiled, her gaze steady on Quinn.

"I'm going to be transparent with you, Ms. Canals: you are who we want. Your experience, your brilliant football mind... Not to mention, your ties to the city. All of our eggs are in the Quinn Canals basket."

Quinn stayed quiet for a moment, letting the words hang in the air. Her mind, usually quick to calculate and assess, was struggling to connect the dots.

Greta smiled, waiting for Quinn to respond. "Should I go on? Or am I completely wasting my time here?"

"I'm sorry, but... this is a very unusual interview," Quinn observed. "I haven't said a word."

Greta smiled, then she chortled a bit. "Correct me if I'm wrong, but... you've been interviewing to be a head coach your entire life, no?"

Quinn had no idea how to respond to that. There was a part of her that was flattered—she appreciated the honesty and directness of Greta's approach, not to mention the respect Greta was showing. But another part of her felt trapped. The Starlings weren't what she had in mind when she envisioned her next job, and definitely not what she thought would be her first head coaching job.

Quinn took a deep breath, her gaze steady as she considered her answer. "I admire your recruitment tactics, and I'm impressed by the efforts of your organization to create a legitimate and competitive club here."

Greta's smile grew, though there was a glimmer of anxiety in her eyes as if she knew what was coming next.

"But..." Quinn continued, her tone firm but polite, "I'm just... I don't think I'm the right fit for what you're building here for the long-term future."

Greta's expression shifted ever so slightly, her professionalism intact but disappointment creeping into her posture. She nodded slowly, clearly not having expected this response.

She quickly ran over in her mind what had happened over the past 30 minutes of this meeting, and she concluded one thing that could've possibly warranted this response from Quinn: "It's the salary, isn't it?" Greta asked, cutting straight to the point.

"Yes," Quinn replied, to the point without a single beat.

Underneath that polished exterior, there was a sharpness in Greta's eyes—an intensity that hinted at the pressure she was under to make the Starlings a success. To this point, Greta's voice was calm and composed, with every word carefully chosen; however, as it felt like she was losing Quinn, she swallowed hard and continued playing to win.

"You will be our head football coach," Greta said, laying all of her cards on the table, "with final say on *all* on-field personnel decisions. And… you'll be the highest-paid coach in the entire league."

Quinn kept her face neutral, though the offer didn't surprise her. She knew she was a big draw, especially for a team like the Starlings in a league like this. They needed her name and her experience. But there was something about this setup that still didn't sit right.

"The annual salary is less than what I make per month in the NFL," Quinn said, matter-of-fact.

Greta didn't miss a beat. She looked right at Quinn, her blue eyes cold but not unkind. "With all due respect, you're no longer in the NFL."

The words hit harder than Quinn expected. She looked down for a moment, letting the truth settle in. She wasn't in the NFL anymore. No matter how much she fought it, no matter how much she tried to deny it, that chapter of her life was closed. She could feel the weight of it pressing on her chest.

Quinn stood abruptly, straightening her shoulders as if trying to shake off the sting of Greta's words. "I'm sorry, Ms. McFly," she said, preparing to leave.

Greta didn't flinch. Instead, she rose to her full height and extended her hand, her expression calm but resolute. "Please, call me Greta. And… so am I."

For a moment, the two women stood in silence, the tension between them palpable. Greta's hand hung in the air, unwavering, her demeanor unshaken by Quinn's hesitance.

Finally, Quinn took Greta's hand, giving it a firm shake before letting go. As she left the building, Greta remained standing tall, her eyes following Quinn as she walked away.

Greta's immediate reaction was one of frustration—frustration at losing a key opportunity for the team, but also at the fact that she couldn't quite convince Quinn of the potential that lay in front of her. Greta had expected some hesitation, after all, the National Flag Football League wasn't the NFL, and Quinn had her sights set on returning to the top pro football league in the world. But still, it stung that Quinn didn't yet see the vision Greta had for the Starlings—where they could go under Quinn's leadership, and how it could be a transformative opportunity for both her as a coach and the team.

Despite losing her number one choice, Greta couldn't sit around dwelling on something she couldn't change. She had a wife and three children, so perhaps she was used to not always getting what she wanted, and with 12 years of marriage under her belt, finding a way to rebound quickly from such personal disappointments was a skill she had mastered. And she would definitely need it now with the season quickly approaching.

So she took a breath to reset, turned, and headed straight back to her office to continue her search for the next Baltimore Starlings' head football coach.

THE FAMILY

The black SUV pulled up in front of a 1920s craftsman-style house in North West Baltimore—the once-charming exterior now showing signs of wear and neglect. The yard, which had likely been pristine at some point, was overgrown with weeds, and the front porch sagged slightly, hinting at years of weathering and disrepair. Quinn stepped out of the SUV and stood for a moment, staring at the house she had once called home. It looked smaller than it did just last year for some reason, and older, like time had passed it by—just like everything else.

As she walked toward the front door, the familiar scent of the neighborhood hit her, a mix of salt and seafood from the harbor in the distance and the earthy smell of city streets. Quinn felt a pang of nostalgia, but it was quickly replaced by a sense of distance. This place, though filled with memories, felt foreign now, like she had left a version of herself here that no longer existed.

Inside the house, the sound of a TV blaring broke the silence. Quinn stepped into the living room, her eyes scanning the space. The house was neat and well-kept, but outdated, with furniture that had clearly been there for decades. The TV cast a harsh glow across the room, but no one was in sight.

"Papa? Mama? You here?" Quinn called out, her voice carrying through the otherwise quiet house.

She suddenly noticed Traci, her mother, sitting quietly in a corner, a cashew-complected Black woman well into her sixties. Her presence was calm, almost ghost-like, as she sat silently, her gaze distant. The years had softened her features, but there was a sadness in her posture, a heaviness that Quinn could feel even from across the room.

Before Quinn could move toward her, a familiar voice called out from behind her.

"Aye! Is that my little girl?"

Pedro "Papa" Canals—jovial, salt of the earth, and full of warmth—appeared out of nowhere, a broad smile lighting up his face. At 66, he still carried himself with the energy of a man much younger, despite the years weighing on him. His skin was a buttery caramel, his once jet-black hair was streaked salt and pepper, and his almond eyes crinkled with genuine joy as he rushed to hug his daughter.

Quinn's mahogany complexion didn't match either of her parents', but she never once questioned the love in their family. Papa wrapped her in a tight embrace and kissed her face over and over as if too much time had passed since their last meeting.

"We miss you," he said, his voice a mix of delight and gentle reproach. "We never see you. You turn the big 3-5 last week, and we don't even get to celebrate with you..."

"There wasn't a celebration," she mumbled under her breath.

But he went on, playfully chastising her: "You just wanna Zoom FaceTime us once a week like we're old roommates you used to know. I don't know. You don't love us anymore–"

"Papa..." Quinn sighed, her voice softening. "Don't say that."

He chuckled, "You haven't changed—always such a serious kid. Lighten up. I'm messing with you."

Before Papa could go on, Traci shifted in her chair, her voice soft and distant. "Who is that?"

"It's Quinn, baby. Your daughter," Papa said, his tone slightly gentler as he glanced at his wife, then back at Quinn.

Quinn felt a tightness in her chest as her mother's confusion sank in. It wasn't the first time this had happened, but it still hurt. It felt worse each time.

Papa continued, trying to fill the silence. "It's not any better since the last time you were here... what was it? Fourth of July?"

Quinn looked down, guilt washing over her. She

hadn't been home as much as she should have been. Football had taken up all of her time—her thoughts, her energy, her life. She felt a twinge of shame as she realized how much she had missed.

Papa reached out, placing his hands on either side of her face, gently lifting her chin so their eyes met. His gaze softened, revealing concern behind his usual cheerfulness. "Are you okay since... everything?"

He had asked this before, but this was the first time he'd get to do so in-person. Perhaps, he figured he'd get a different answer by looking her in the eyes.

Quinn hesitated, her throat tightening as she tried to find the words. She wanted to say something real, something honest, but instead, she offered the safest response she could. "I'm okay, Papa."

Papa studied her for a moment, his expression skeptical, but he didn't push. Traditionally, Traci was the one who would press Quinn for real answers, not letting her get away with hiding behind succinct statements that she hoped were enough to shut up the questions. But Traci was available for her usual loving interrogation, so Papa just accepted Quinn's answer, both of them knowing full well he didn't actually believe it.

He released her and moved toward the kitchen, his voice light again. "You want some tea? What are you doing in town? You didn't call or nothing."

Quinn followed him, feeling the warmth of the house, the familiarity of her father's presence.

"Yeah, I'll take some jasmine. And I know. It was last minute... A job interview thing, but... it's not going to work out. I'm leaving in the morning."

Papa nodded as he placed a mug filled with water into the microwave. Quinn frowned at the sight of this.

"Why are you warming water in the microwave?" she asked with her brows furrowed.

Papa chuckled softly. "Oh. Stove's broken, mija. But it's okay. I've just been grilling more."

Quinn glanced around the kitchen, noticing the little things. The house still held together, but it was clear her parents weren't keeping up with everything like they used to. Her brows knitted with concern, but she kept her thoughts to herself.

Papa, ever the optimist, waved off any worries as he changed the subject. "Listen, we're about to head out on our daily walk, you know, gotta get our steps in." He smiled, then added, "You haven't seen your brothers yet–"

"I'm going to," Quinn said, cutting him off gently, though unsure if she'd have the time or energy.

Papa's smile brightened. "You should. Before you leave, please. They wanna see you. Drew is running the business now."

Quinn's eyes widened slightly in surprise. "You finally let him take over, huh?"

Papa's face softened, a mix of pride and sadness settling in his eyes. "Aye, if your mama wasn't like this, you know I would never leave that place. I gotta be here for her so..."

He trailed off, his voice heavy with the unspoken weight of responsibility. He walked back over to Quinn, placing his hands on either side of her face again, a gesture of comfort and love.

"It's so good to see you, mi amore," he said, his tone warm and genuine. "But you know how to make your own tea."

He kissed her forehead and went back to bustling around the kitchen.

"Where's mine?"

Quinn's head quickly whipped around to look back at Traci, sitting there with her arms outreached, waiting to receive the same treatment Pedro just got.

Quinn swallowed, a bit taken off-guard as she stepped toward her mother, who stood up to wrap her arms around her more tightly. Quinn returned the embrace, instantly being thrust back to her preschool self when those hugs were everything—the only thing that could calm her down, cure her fears, or get her to sleep at night.

She exhaled. She was safe here. She could stay in those arms forever. But after a moment, Traci gently pulled back, looked at her with a soft and uncertain glare, and said, "Nice to meet you, young lady."

Quinn's heart clenched at the words, but she forced a smile and held her composure, as she replied, "Nice to meet you too... mama."

* * *

The distinct fragrance of flavored spices and fresh fish hit Quinn in the face as she stepped into Canals' Crab Shack. It was just as busy as she remembered, the small restaurant packed with customers from the counter to the door. The sound of sizzling pots and clattering dishes filled the air, along with the low murmur of impatient customers checking their watches and phones. The chaotic energy of the place was familiar, but something felt off. The place looked... unorganized, clunky, as if the efficiency that once defined it had slipped away.

Quinn stood out of sight by the door for a moment, watching it all unfold. A few workers lounged near the kitchen, chatting casually as bags of food sat waiting on the counter for pick-up. The flow was off, and it was clear to her in seconds.

Her eyes scanned the room, searching for a familiar face before landing on Big Mase—formally named Mason, but somehow those two syllables just felt like too much to say—the kitchen leader, darting around as usual, seemingly doing everything himself while the other staff moved at a slower, lazier pace. He hadn't changed much—still tall, still stocky, still wearing his signature Orioles cap that never moved despite his quick movements that showed his years of experience in the kitchen. Although he was only 40, he'd been working in the place since Quinn was a teen. She could see the strain in his eyes, the weight of keeping the place together.

"Quinn!" Mase's face lit up as he spotted her, wiping his hands on a towel before hurrying over to properly greet her. "Hey, what are you doing here, girl?"

Before she could respond, he was already coming in for a hug, so Quinn obliged with reluctance. "Just making sure the place hasn't burned down," she responded.

Mase chuckled as he backed up to get a good look at her, but the weariness in his posture didn't go unnoticed by Quinn. She glanced around, her brow furrowing as she watched the workers moving sluggishly, chatting instead of working. "Where's my brother?"

Mase looked around the room, his expression shifting slightly. "Hell if I know. He's around here somewhere."

He turned to one of the workers, his tone quick and authoritative. "Drop the next batch and take those shrimp out of the steamer."

Quinn's eyes flicked to the steamer, noticing its blinking light. Her face tightened with disapproval. "The steamer should have a timer."

Mase sighed, his shoulders slumping slightly. "Yeah, well... it's broken so..."

Quinn shook her head, already calculating the inefficiency. "So you need a timer. One minute under and they're too fleshy. A minute over and they're hard to peel and tough to chew. They have to be just right."

Mase swallowed hard, clearly aware that Quinn knew the operation inside and out. He nodded with respect, taking in her words as she moved toward a machine that had been blinking since she arrived. Quinn hit the button to turn it off and opened the top, letting a waft of steam billow out into the kitchen.

"These crabs are overcooked," Quinn said, her tone flat but firm. "People are waiting on average twenty-three minutes. That's eleven minutes longer than they should be."

Without waiting for a response, Quinn grabbed a pair of tongs hanging from the wall and used them to pull out a crab from the pot. She laid it on the table, flipping it onto its back.

"Most women use a knife to open 'em," Mase quipped.

Ignoring that comment, she proceeded to tear off the T-shaped part of the shell that indicated a male crab, and then she pulled the body apart, revealing...

"You see that?" Quinn pointed at the stringy, almost dry crab meat. "This is supposed to be juicy, plump, moist, right? Not stringy like this."

She pulled out a piece of meat and tasted it, grimacing at the tough texture. Mase, watching closely, swallowed nervously as Quinn handed him a piece. He tasted it, his expression neutral, but he knew what she was getting at.

"It's a little hard to get out too," Quinn continued, her voice unyielding. "They can be forgiving, but with that line out there, there's no reason these should've sat in here for this long. Smells a little funky too. You can't sell this."

Mase nodded slowly, clearly overwhelmed but unable to argue with her assessment. His respect for Quinn was evident in the way he shrank slightly under her gaze, knowing she was right.

Without a smile, she added, "Most men know how to steam crabs without a timer."

He smiled: touché.

Quinn's eyes shifted to the workers lounging near the counter, moving sluggishly between tasks. She didn't hesitate. "You, you, and you. Come here."

The three workers glanced up, confused, and took their time moving toward her. They'd never met her before, so they were unsure whether she was even talking to them. But Quinn's patience thinned because they weren't moving fast enough, and her voice sharpened as she waved them over. "Hustle! Quickly! Come on."

Now, they rushed to stand in front of her, lining up side by side as if awaiting orders. Quinn sized them up quickly, her mind already calculating where each of them could be most efficient.

"You're going to swap positions," she said, pointing to the shortest of the three. "You: you're great with people, so you should be the one they get when they're placing orders. You're on the register."

She turned to the tall one next. "You know the menu well, so you can fill and bag the orders quickly."

Finally, she pointed to the middle one, her gaze steady. "And you, you're new. You move too slowly and you talk too much. You're going to be serving now. Okay, hurry back to your places."

The workers quickly scurried back to their new positions, and within moments, the flow of the restaurant began to move more smoothly. Quinn and Mase watched as the line started moving faster, orders being taken and filled with more efficiency.

Mase let out a small sigh of relief, nodding in silent appreciation for Quinn's help.

But just as things were settling into place, a voice cut through the bustle from behind them.

"Yo, what the fuck you doing?"

Quinn turned to see Drew, her brother, standing at the entrance of the kitchen, his face twisted in annoyance. Drew, at 38, looked every bit the part of someone who had never fully let go of his rebellious youth—a white rapper type, with dyed blonde hair, covered in tattoos, with a vape pen in hand, and a countenance hardened by years of taking shortcuts. He stared at Quinn, clearly displeased with her asserting herself in his territory.

Mase, sensing the tension, quietly slipped away, leaving the siblings to face each other.

Growing up, Drew always looked out for Quinn,

even when she didn't know it. In fact, most of the time, she didn't know it—always in her own world. Academically, she picked up on things quicker than most—details, numbers, patterns—but she seldom decoded emotional messages the way in which they were intended, which frustrated most people. And with kids, especially teenagers, this caused them to just want to fight her.

She never fought. But Drew did. And being three years older than her, his seniority over most of her would-be bullies solved problems she didn't even know she had.

She, on the other hand, just saw her brother as rash, reckless, and recalcitrant. So despite his constant protection of her, they didn't always get along.

Like Quinn, Traci and Pedro had adopted Drew—their second after fostering him. Of course, they had concerns about what it would look like for a Black and Puerto Rican couple to have a child of Scottish/Irish descent, but they did it anyway, raising him from age two as if he was their own.

With all of their kids, they emphasized academics, so Drew made his presence known in the classroom, but they also encouraged whatever else the kids gravitated toward. For Drew, it was painting, cooking, and lacrosse. In fact, he went to Duke on a lacrosse scholarship, but his college career, unfortunately, only lasted three semesters. He dropped out after getting reprimanded for violating their possession of alcohol policy, subsequently losing his athletic scholarship, which he insisted was taken away because a lingering knee injury hindered his playing time. Either way, he couldn't afford to stay at the school.

He returned home where Quinn—the only girl—had become the sole beneficiary of their parent's attention and affection. He couldn't blame her, though, for the change in the way they looked at him now. He had disappointed them gravely, so perhaps it was his own insecurities that made him believe that they wanted him to be more like Quinn.

Quinn was their youngest and the only child they adopted without having fostered at any point. Drew, being the middle child, accepted her but noticed the loss of attention he got once she was around. Although her skin was much darker than either of their parents', Drew still felt like they could more easily avoid questions about whether Quinn was theirs or not, and this made him feel even more like an outsider.

So, despite his love for his baby sister, he might've harbored some resentment. Watching her make history as a "first" in the world to do something made him both extremely proud and also a bit competitive. He wanted to have a thing that people could be proud of him for, and he thought that maybe the restaurant could be that thing.

When she showed up trying to impose herself

on his thing, his system, his way of doing stuff? This understandably angered him. He neither wanted nor needed help from her, and he wanted to make sure and let her know this. So, instead of having this conversation in the kitchen of his restaurant, Drew led her outside.

"What are you doing here?" he asked.

"I had an interview with a–"

"No, I mean… fucking *here*," he said, emphasizing the restaurant.

"Dad said you wanted to see me," she answered with a slight upward inflection as if maybe now she was asking him rather than asserting this as a fact.

Drew used this moment to take a long, slow, squinted-eyed drag from his vape, leaving Quinn hanging, as if to say (without saying) that what "Dad said" wasn't the truth. In fact, he decided that he just wasn't going to give her a response to that statement at all.

"So you've been home," he deduced. "You've seen the house."

She knew what he was implying; she had seen it for herself—the real attention the place needed, not the patchwork that had kept it upright the last decade or so.

"You know Papa. He's proud. He won't let me do anything to help…"

Drew chuckled. "Oh, so *now* you let people get a say in what the fuck you do or don't do?"

She hadn't thought about this in that way. When she first started making big money about three years ago, she wanted to do what every kid who finds financial success wants to do: buy her parents a new house. But they insisted that they loved their home—the only place they'd ever lived—and wanted to stay where they were. Pedro was still running his family's 50-year-old business and Traci was still teaching. They didn't want it to appear as if they thought they were above the people they spent all their time with.

Even when their kids threw out the idea of a renovation, Pedro shut them down. When something would break, instead of asking for help, he'd fix it if he could or just live with it broken—like the stove—until he could figure something out himself.

So, Quinn let go of the idea of trying to insert herself into their living situation. The fact that she normally imposed her will on people but was choosing to sit this one out was mind-boggling to Drew—another reason for an eye-roll and head shake.

Again, he sucked on his vape pen, his brows furrowed as he glared at Quinn. "So you figured you'd just show up out of nowhere and start running shit *here*?"

Quinn's face remained calm, though her voice carried a sharp edge. "Do you know what our Yelp rating looks like?"

Drew's expression shifted to one of confusion, as if the question itself was absurd. He squinted at her, trying to gauge if she was serious. "Yelp? Man, get outta here with that."

But Quinn wasn't backing down. She pulled out her phone, reading from the reviews she had already checked before coming in. "We were always a top spot in the city for seafood—the best for blue crabs alone. Winning was everything. Now?"

She scrolled down, her tone colder as she quoted one of the reviews aloud. "'Service is slow. Food is okay but not worth the wait.'"

Drew shifted uncomfortably, his eyes narrowing as Quinn's words hit home. He didn't respond, but the truth was written all over his face.

"That's the consensus," Quinn continued, not giving him a chance to deflect. "We're down to a 4.1 rating. That's... very average."

Drew's irritation flared, and he put out his vape with a frustrated huff. "We? Worry about your own fuckin' business, yo. I got a job to do."

The jab landed, but Quinn remained calm, watching him with a level gaze as he turned to head back into the kitchen.

"Love you," she said in the most flat, routine, obligatory—maybe even sarcastic—way, although she did actually mean it.

He responded by throwing up his middle finger over his shoulder as he disappeared through the door. She simply shook her head, not reading anything into his mean response. She knew he loved her.

Quinn could feel the weight of his resentment though, but she wasn't going to let this restaurant situation slide. Drew was running things now, but if he didn't shape up, Canals' Crab Shack wouldn't last. She made a mental note to check up on him, whether he wanted it or not.

Before she finished fully processing her thoughts, a customer, an older man in his sixties, stopped by the door, looking at her with curiosity. "Hey, ain't you that girl coach from the NFL that got arrested?"

The words stung, but Quinn nodded politely before turning away. She could feel the judgment and the weight of the past hovering over her wherever she went.

* * *

"Running waste management for the entire city isn't a glamorous job," the woman said. "But we're essential workers that keep the city running smoothly…"

As the trash lady spoke confidently about her work, her voice carried across the quiet lot as she detailed the importance of her job—a topic Quinn's eldest brother, Gabe, had clearly found compelling enough to center his project around.

To finish fulfilling the obligation she had made to her father, Quinn arrived on the scene at the sanitation department's parking lot just in time to catch the last few moments of the final interview of the day. She spotted Gabe leading the small crew of five students, his casual way of dressing made him blend in with them.

Gabe was Quinn's eldest brother, her senior by six years, and unlike his sister, everyone who knew him liked him—a natural people-person who made friends everywhere he went. A Howard University grad, now film teacher at Maryland Institute College of Art, he was known for his laid-back charm and creative mind. At 41, Gabe carried himself with the easy confidence of someone who has always marched to his own beat. Short, newly twisted locs atop a tall and lean frame, he dressed in a way that blended well into artsy settings—vintage band tees, jeans, and an assortment of accessories and rings that hinted at his free-spirited nature.

Quinn never admitted this to anyone, but Gabe might've been her best friend if he wasn't already her brother. The energy in Gabe's art world was different from Quinn's so whenever she was around him, she just felt looser, freer, less defined by competition and wins and losses.

Gabe was the first child Traci and Pedro welcomed into their family. As a young couple—an elementary school teacher and a line cook at his family's Crab Shack respectively—they weren't thinking about kids. In fact, they hadn't even discussed marriage when the situation presented itself for them to be temporary guardians for the recently orphaned son of one of

Pedro's coworkers who died of a drug overdose.

Pedro knew the four-year-old boy, who had spent time around the restaurant when his mother couldn't find a sitter, but he didn't know much. He knew that the boy's father—a white, married trucker who planted a seed on a trip through Baltimore one winter—had zero interest in knowing, let alone raising, a little Black boy. So Pedro knew that the boy's next stop would be the system.

Oh, and he knew that the boy liked to be called "Gabe." That was the extent of his knowledge of Gabe's life.

Pedro came home one day and asked his live-in girlfriend if "this kid" could stay with them for a while until some things got sorted out. After hearing his story, Traci didn't hesitate or even question, "Why us?" Perhaps that's when Pedro knew—or finally admitted—it was time that he let Traci make an honest man out of him.

What started out as a temporary thing eventually turned into a concerted effort to make themselves Gabe's parents, which meant Pedro had to do more than just admit it was time; he had to actually make things official with Traci. And so, he did.

Traci and Pedro never had kids of their own, although it wasn't because of a lack of trying. But constant miscarriages made them feel like they were just supposed to be parents in another way, so they created their family as they saw fit.

So today, Quinn watched the documentary interview scene in admiration of her brother, while standing at a distance in the parking lot of the trash facility. She respected Gabe's passion for his work, but she never quite understood how he could be so absorbed in random stories like this—stories that, in her eyes, didn't really move the needle. Yet, he always found a way to make them seem important, even beautiful, in their own way.

Since they were right near everything good, once they were done, Gabe treated his team and Quinn to tacos at a nearby food truck where they could eat outside.

The truck sat parked near the busy edge of Baltimore's business district, its faded yellow paint peeling slightly under the afternoon sun. Around it, Gabe's students crowded into outdoor seating, laughing and chatting as they enjoyed their food. Quinn sat across from her brother at one of the wobbly tables, the truck's sizzling grill providing a background soundtrack to their conversation.

Gabe took a bite of his taco, gesturing with it as he spoke. "It's a documentary. I decided to start this year and let the students get practical experience on a long-form project. They'll get IMDb credit and everything."

Quinn, unimpressed, grabbed a tortilla chip from her plate and popped it into her mouth. "They can't eat IMDB credit. They're working. Pay them."

Gabe grinned and casually reached over to steal one of her chips, undeterred by her frankness. "I'll pay them."

It was typical of Gabe to brush off her practical concerns with his carefree charm. With his "meet people where they are" personality, Gabe and Quinn always got along rather nicely. He didn't offend easily, so her curtness and bluntness was never taken personally. Quinn respected his passion, but their worlds had always been so different—hers, driven by results and strategy; his, by creativity and spontaneity. Still, there was an ease between them, even when they didn't see eye to eye.

Gabe leaned in, his expression lighting up with an idea. "Aye, you should be in it. I think you'd be perfect, actually."

Quinn squirmed silently, not interested in this proposal, despite having zero idea what the thing was even about.

Gabe swallowed a bite of his food before continuing. "The documentary? You are exactly what the story is about."

Quinn immediately recoiled at the thought. She wasn't someone who craved the spotlight—at least, not the kind that came with random personal exposure.

But Gabe's enthusiasm bubbled over as he explained, "I'm serious. It's about women dominating in traditional male spaces. Your whole NFL thing…"

The mention of the NFL sent a sharp pang through Quinn's stomach. Her face hardened, and she cut him off before he could go any further. "I'm not in the NFL... anymore."

The words came out more bitter than she'd intended, but Gabe didn't seem fazed. He looked at her with the same softness he always had, like he saw more in her than just her professional success.

"Yeah, but you were," he said, his voice quieter now. "And you were... *are* great. You *are* a *great* coach."

Quinn's eyes dropped to her plate, her throat tightening as the weight of his compliment settled over her. She wasn't used to hearing praise like that, not from someone who actually meant it. Her career had always been about pushing forward, about winning. There wasn't room for reflection, for acknowledging the cost of what she had achieved—and lost.

Seeing her discomfort, Gabe leaned back in his chair, giving her a little space. But he wasn't done making his case. "Listen, no one can take away what you achieved, Quinn. Ever. This doc... it explores what that experience was like. Do it. Please."

Quinn shook her head, trying to put distance between herself and the idea. "Honestly? I think it's a stupid concept. It's terribly boring, and nobody wants to watch that, so... no, I'm not going to be a part of it. But good luck."

Gabe smiled, knowing that his little sister's defensive walls were up, but not taking it personally.

He had learned long ago how to handle Quinn's brusque manner. It was her way, and there was no need to expect anything different.

After a brief pause, Gabe shifted gears, his tone casual but with a hint of mischief. "You know... Drew called me." He didn't bother revealing the details of their conversation. All he did was warn Quinn: "You must'a forgot, he's a lot more sensitive than I am."

Quinn looked up, her expression of curiosity masking the eye-roll she wanted to give at the mention of their historically predictable other brother. "Dad needs a manager for the restaurant, or I give it seven... nine months tops. Drew's not a manager."

It was the truth, plain and simple. Quinn didn't believe Drew had the discipline to run Canals' Crab Shack the way their father had. She had seen it the moment she walked into the restaurant. It was only a matter of time before things fell apart.

Quinn glanced at her phone, noticing the time. The day was slipping away faster than she'd expected. "I gotta run," she said, pushing her chair back and standing up.

Gabe, surprised by how quickly the conversation was ending, began wiping his mouth... "Wait, you... How long are you in town? We barely got to talk."

Quinn offered a half-hearted smile as she gathered her things. "I'll call you. It's just... I have a standing thing I do every Thursday. I can't miss it. But I'll call you, okay?"

Gabe sighed, disappointed but understanding. He knew his sister well enough to know when he wasn't going to change her mind. "Okay, don't forget to call."

Quinn gave him a brief nod before turning and walking away, her mind already shifting to the next thing on her list. As much as she wanted to stay, to connect with her brother, the weight of her past and her present was pulling her in different directions.

THE MENTOR

B ack in her hotel room at the Four Seasons, Quinn settled into the sleek, modern space. The minimalist decor felt nothing like home, but she barely noticed. Her mind was elsewhere. Still turning over the events of the day, she had other things to focus on—her Thursday night meeting, the one routine she hadn't let slip, even as everything else in her life had unraveled.

Quinn sat down at the polished desk, her MacBook glowing in front of her as she prepared for the FaceTime call. The room around her was still, the city sounds muffled by the thick glass windows. The TV flickered quietly in the background, offering a distraction she didn't need. She could hear a pundit's excited voice reporting on upcoming NFL draft prospects.

"And he played in a pro-style offense at Wisconsin. He's expected to go number one in next year's draft..." Mina Kimes' voice faded in and out as Quinn

barely registered the words. Having football news broadcasting like white noise was a habit.

This time, she decided to turn it to something else, anything else, just to get the NFL off her mind, at least for the time being.

The local news happened to be talking sports too, but she left it there, giving up. *"And local Olympian, Alana Ari, has opted to reevaluate her 100-meter dreams, taking the year off to consider her future in the sport. She might not have been fast enough to qualify, but she will be making sure your deliveries arrive on time..."*

Quinn finally refocused. As she tapped the screen and waited for it to connect to someone on the other end, she thought back on that night at Dave & Busters a few months ago as Mike said: "You'll have the rum. It's a splash. What's the worst that can happen?"

Quinn was not herself that evening at the bar-arcade. At least, not the version of herself she had carefully crafted to present to the world. No, at that bar, she leaned back in her chair, laughing—genuinely laughing—her posture loose, her usually sharp eyes slightly glazed over... The once intimidating, disciplined, no-nonsense coach had been replaced by someone who seemed carefree, unbothered, and ready to enjoy the moment—a personality shift that was definitely brought on by the pretty blue liquid she kept drinking.

She waved her now-empty glass in the air as the waiter passed by—her voice louder than usual and more brash than necessary. "I'll have another one of these… goddamn things," she called out, flashing a smile at the others sitting around the table.

Turning back to the group, she continued, her words flowing easily, her hands gesturing as she spoke. "So I says, 'If you knew all that, you could've told him before we got here.'"

Sarah, still shaking her head in disbelief, looked at her with wide eyes. "You said that to the president of the Raiders? You're fucking crazy, bro."

Quinn grinned, feeling lighter than she had in years. This was what it felt like to let go. To stop caring so much.

The sound of a voice, dripping with disdain, cut through the laughter at the table. "No wonder you're all unemployed. A bunch of non-coaching ass losers."

Quinn's smile faltered slightly, and she turned toward the source of the interruption. It was the same "fan" from earlier—the one who had muttered something under his breath when she first arrived. He was leaning against a nearby table, arms crossed, a smug grin plastered across his face.

Quinn narrowed her eyes, feeling the alcohol buzz in her head as she responded, her voice playful but edged with irritation. "Hey, aren't you supposed to be keeping it moving? Asshole."

Her laugh came easy, and the others joined in,

their amusement obvious. The guy, however, wasn't so amused.

"Yeah, well, at least I got a job, girly," he sneered, his voice loud enough for everyone around them to hear. "You're a hack. Overrated. An embarrassment as an OC, losing every goddamn week on national TV. The only reason the NFL even hired you is because you check all the boxes."

The laughter around the table quieted. Quinn's grin faded as the words landed harder than she'd expected. She felt the familiar weight of them settling in her chest, the sting of every whisper, every article that had questioned her legitimacy as a coach.

The fan wasn't done. He leaned in, his voice dripping with mockery. "Face it, you're just a woke DEI write-off."

Quinn stood up, her muscles tensing, a surge of anger coursing through her body. Mike jumped up beside her, hands out in a calming gesture, trying to keep the situation from escalating. But the fanboy just laughed, backing away with a cocky smirk.

"You should've heard them before you got here. Let's be honest, the real reason you don't got a job is because... NO. ONE. LIKES. YOU." He spat the words out, each one a blow to her pride.

Quinn stood frozen, the words echoing in her mind. No one likes you. It was something she had always tried to ignore, something that she knew lingered behind every interaction, every failed interview. But hearing it said so plainly, so publicly, hit differently.

The guy turned and started to walk away, laughing as if he'd won some small victory.

For a moment, time slowed. Quinn's eyes followed him, her blood boiling. She felt her fists clench at her sides, the anger coiling tighter in her chest. Out of the corner of her eye, she spotted a worker passing by with a cart filled with mini footballs. Without thinking, Quinn snatched one from the cart, her fingers tightening around the familiar texture of the ball.

In a flash, she made her move.

It was a spot-on Mahomes impersonation—a swift, sharp release, and the ball was sailing through the air, cutting through the crowd with lethal accuracy.

But Quinn's aim, though exact, didn't take into account the guy dropping his phone at that exact moment and having to bend down to pick it up just as the ball was set to make contact. So, instead of hitting him, the ball cut through the crowd and smashed right into the face of a young girl standing just a few feet behind him.

For a moment, the world seemed to freeze. Then, in horrifying clarity, the girl's nose burst, blood spraying instantly across her face. Her mother, Caitlin, screamed, rushing to her daughter's side, trying desperately to stop the bleeding.

The girl stumbled backward, her hands covering her face as tears streamed down her cheeks. The sound of her cry pierced through the noise of the arcade.

Quinn's heart dropped into her stomach.

Everything moved in slow motion... The shocked gasps of the crowd... The sudden commotion as people rushed to help... And Quinn—frozen in place, staring in horror at the unintended damage she had caused. The ball, which had been meant for the fanboy's smug head, had instead found the face of an innocent child.

The girl's blood-streaked face filled Quinn's vision, and guilt slammed into her like a freight train.

And that's what led to a mug shot that night, which made her a national news story, which led to the potential first female head football coach in NFL history becoming nothing more than a laughing stock. A dream deferred.

She felt so awful that she showed up at the kid's house later that week with a gift bag and balloons. When her mother, Caitlin, an otherwise pleasant 40-year-old white woman with long brown hair and bluish eyes identical to her daughter's, opened the door, everything Quinn wanted to say seemed to float away.

For a moment, they stood there in silence as Caitlin, who now held an unforgiving disdain for Quinn, waited for her to explain why she was there.

"Listen, Mrs. McCoy, I just want to apologize

again to you, and especially to your daughter for... the incident. I ah... heard she was a um... a big Eagles fan? Well, I... I got her a few things here–"

With an exasperated sigh, Caitlin decided to comfort her by revealing, "We're not pressing charges, Ms. Canals. The hospital bill was... more than generous. Thank you."

And she started to close the door, but Quinn had more.

"Also, I know that she wants to play quarterback. It... I was on your IG page. You had a little picture of her playing at... Nevermind," she said, stopping short of revealing that she'd been stalking Caitlin online. "If you're okay with it, I'd be open to, say, giving her a few tips about the game. It may help... in some way. I donno..."

Caitlin studied her. Quinn's face pleaded for forgiveness, so Caitlin surrendered. She sighed and stepped back, opening the door.

"Come in."

So tonight, Quinn sat in her hotel room at the Four Seasons waiting for her FaceTime call to connect, and when the ringing stopped and the image appeared, it revealed a brown-haired, blue-eyed white girl smiling into the camera: 12-year-old Nyad McCoy.

Nyad's face was bright and excited, her thick hair slightly messy, as if she'd just finished a long day. In the background, Quinn could see her room cluttered with NFL memorabilia—posters, jerseys, and helmets, filling nearly every inch of wall space.

"Hey, Quinn!" Nyad exclaimed, her eyes already lit up with excitement as if she'd been anticipating this call since the one a week ago.

"Nyad, hey. Good to see you," Quinn replied, her voice soft but warm, the tension in her shoulders loosening slightly at the sight of the familiar face.

"Look what I got," Nyad said, proudly holding up a Lamar Jackson rookie card. The card shimmered in the light, its value clear even through the screen.

Quinn's eyebrows lifted, genuinely impressed.

"His rookie card. I got it in a trade," Nyad added with a grin.

"What'd you have to give up?" Quinn asked, leaning in a bit.

"A Justin Herbert and a Tua rookie," Nyad said, still grinning ear to ear. "But Lamar is the man, so I think I won that one."

Quinn nodded, agreeing. "Statistically, you're right. Through his first 76 starts, Lamar Jackson had the exact same record as Tom Brady of 57 and 19. He had a 6.1% touchdown rate with a .165 EPA to play ratio, making him one of the most efficient QBs in NFL history."

Nyad burst out laughing, her giggles filling the silence of the room. "You're so weird."

Quinn's lips curled into a half-smile, a little awkward.

Nyad's laugh faded as she tilted her head, curiosity in her voice. "Where are you?"

Quinn glanced around the room as if just realizing her surroundings. "Oh. Home. Well, a hotel in Baltimore. I had a ah... job interview. They flew me out."

Nyad's eyes widened. "Did you get it?"

Quinn hesitated, her fingers lightly tapping the edge of the laptop. "Ah... actually yeah, but... I turned it down. The Baltimore Starlings. It's a... flag football team."

"I've never played flag football. What's that like?" Nyad asked, genuinely curious.

Quinn's eyes narrowed with realization. "I've never played it either."

Nyad looked thoughtful for a moment before speaking again. "Well, it sounds like fun. You need a job, so why'd you turn that one down?"

Quinn exhaled, trying to find the right words. "Because..."

She paused, looking for the best way to explain. "Let's just say it pays a fraction of what I made in the NFL, so it just won't... accommodate my standard of living."

Nyad furrowed her brow as if trying to work out the logic behind it. "Oh. I get it. But... why don't you just stay with your mom and dad? That way, you won't have to worry about paying bills. You would save a bunch of money, so it'll make up for it. And then, if I was you, I would find something about the job that motivates me more than the money."

Quinn listened quietly as Nyad's words hit her. For all her youth, Nyad had a way of seeing things clearly, without the baggage that weighed Quinn down.

Nyad continued, her voice filled with the enthusiasm only a kid could have. "So like, for instance... I'm trying out for the football team. I'll be the only girl. But I have the courage to do it because I'm confident in my knowledge of the game. Why? Because of you. You're a good teacher."

Quinn's heart squeezed at the words, and she sat back, considering what Nyad had said. The simple wisdom of it resonated.

"So I think... maybe you should take the job," Nyad added, her voice full of determination. "You'll totally inspire others to try new stuff they have no idea how to do. Then maybe they'll take risks like playing football like me!"

Quinn stared at the screen, the weight of her decision pressing harder now. "The money is just one reason," she said, her voice quieter. "The real reason is..."

She met Nyad's gaze on the screen, speaking earnestly. "I'll look stupid."

Nyad's face twisted in confusion. "What do you mean?"

Quinn swallowed, trying to explain something

she barely understood herself. "If I do this, it's a step in the wrong direction. It makes me look desperate. I won't be taken seriously in the pro football world... anymore."

For a moment, the two sat in silence, the weight of Quinn's words hanging between them.

Nyad broke the quiet with a laugh, her eyes twinkling mischievously. "After you busted my face, I had to go to school with a big bandage on my nose. And it was picture week!"

Quinn couldn't help but chuckle at the memory, though it still pained her. Nyad continued, giggling. "I looked so stupid. But... my friend Gracie, she got her first period and had to go home, so she didn't even get to take her pictures, which was so tragic. But I just think... we all kinda look stupid sometimes."

Quinn smiled softly, nodding in agreement. "Yeah, I guess we do."

Nyad's face grew thoughtful again. "And sometimes when I'm doing my homework, I'll go get a snack, and when I come back, I'm totally, like, refreshed or whatever. I see the whole assignment more clearly. Maybe that's what'll happen to you. Be away from the NFL, then come back better."

Quinn stared at the screen, Nyad's words sinking in. The simple wisdom of it struck her harder than anything else had in weeks.

Nyad's words hung in the air, filling the quiet space of Quinn's hotel room. The bright city lights outside seemed distant now, like the world beyond these walls didn't matter. For a moment, Quinn just stared at the screen, her mind turning over Nyad's simple, honest advice. There was a wisdom in the girl's words, something that cut through all the noise and self-doubt Quinn had been wrestling with for weeks.

The metaphor that the kid had just broken down for her was something that was always lost on Quinn. When she sought answers, she needed them clear and straightforward, or else she struggled to see how they would benefit her or solve her problem. Finding the intangible or even spiritual benefit was too ethereal for her comprehension. She didn't read between lines very well.

***

Snow swirled through the air, carried by the sharp, cold wind. Baltimore was different here— its streets deserted, its familiar noises replaced by a strange, eerie silence. The snow crunched under Quinn's shoes as she walked, the flakes sticking to her dark hair and melting against her skin. She wasn't sure how long she had been walking, but the city felt both familiar and alien, like a place half-remembered from a distant memory.

Ahead of her, lying half-buried in the snow, she noticed something—a fedora. She bent down and picked it up, her fingers brushing away the frost. It felt solid in her hands, yet out of place in this strange version of the city.

Quinn straightened up and looked around. That's when she noticed a figure up ahead—a man, standing alone in the snow. As she approached, her heart began to race, a glimmer of recognition stirring deep inside her. The closer she got, the more she began to realize who it was.

She stopped in front of him, holding out the fedora.

"You're... you're..." Quinn stammered, her breath visible in the freezing air.

The man smiled, his face warm and familiar to Quinn. It was him—her idol, her hero, the architect of modern football, Paul Brown. This was the guy from many of Quinn's first books on football—the founder and the first head coach of both the Cleveland Browns and the Cincinnati Bengals. With the Browns—his namesake—he created one of the most dominant teams in pro football during the 1940s and 50s, winning seven titles in 12 seasons. Then, after he was inducted into the Pro Football Hall of Fame, he founded the Bengals and coached them for several seasons.

Paul Brown was one of the greatest football minds of his time (nay, of all time)—a tactician who revolutionized the game with his innovative coaching techniques and strategic genius. He was the first to use game film to study opponents, developed what's known as the playbook, and created the detailed scouting report. He also pioneered the use of in-game radio communication between coaches and quarterbacks, a practice that is standard today.

His influence on the sport extended beyond his own coaching career; many of his former assistants, like Bill Walsh, went on to become legendary coaches in their own right. Paul Brown might be the most influential figure in the history of American football.

Since Pedro was a Cleveland Browns fan, Quinn possessed an unusual amount of Browns gear and knowledge as a kid. And though she took a lot away from those books that strengthened her interest in the game overall, the parts that stuck with her and stayed in her heart were the stories of Paul Brown.

So when her eyes landed on the dark brown ones held by the 6'1" middle-aged white guy who had apparently lost his fedora to the wind, she knew exactly who she was looking at. And even still, she couldn't believe it.

His sharp gaze gleamed as he nicely took the hat from her outstretched hand, nodding his thanks.

"I'm here... for you," he said, his voice steady and reassuring, just as she had always imagined it.

Quinn swallowed hard, her heart pounding in her chest. "The reason why I even do what I do, the way I do it... is you," she admitted, her voice almost breaking with the weight of the words. "You're the architect—the reason football coaching is the exact science it is today."

Paul Brown smiled again, gently placing the fedora back on his head.

"So I take it you're here to help me?" she asked, her voice wavering with hope.

Brown chuckled softly, shaking his head. "Help you? No. Believe it or not, kid... you don't need my help."

Confusion and desperation danced across her face. She was meeting her hero, though under the strangest of circumstances. Why wouldn't he be the one to guide her, to show her the way forward?

Paul's voice softened as he stepped closer. "I visit all the greats." He shrugged, adding a half explanation: "Sorta been my thing since about 1992..."

Quinn blinked, trying to process what he was saying. "Wait a minute. 'The greats?'"

The snow stopped with the flakes hanging motionless in the air around them. Paul smiled knowingly, as if her confusion was exactly what he expected. He took a step closer to her, chuckling softly.

"Belichick after Cleveland. That whole 'napkin thing' he did in New York in 2000? I might've had something to do with that. There was Reid after the Eagles in 2013. Harbaugh in '15 after the 9ers... Actually, I still see Jim every now and then. Loves to talk, that one."

Quinn's mind reeled. She felt like she was

teetering on the edge of something, unsure of what it all meant.

Brown's eyes gleamed with amusement. "In fact," he continued, his voice dropping to a conspiratorial whisper, "Jim's the one who suggested I show up earlier for my next one."

Quinn felt a lump form in her throat, her mouth suddenly dry. She swallowed hard and looked up at him, her voice trembling slightly as she asked the question she wasn't sure she was ready to hear the answer to.

"Earlier... for what?"

Paul Brown's smile softened into something more serious, his eyes meeting hers with a steady, reassuring gaze. "Everyone needs coaching, Canals. Even great coaches. Especially the great ones."

The words hit her like a punch to the chest. She had spent so long trying to prove something, to the world and to herself, that she hadn't considered two possibilities: 1. That the greats—those she admired most—needed coaching; and 2. That she was one of them.

"I can't get you there. You're gonna do that on your own," Brown continued, his tone kind but firm. "But you know, being great... it's lonely. So I'll be here with you so you're not so alone."

Quinn's eyes filled with tears she hadn't expected. The truth in his words sank in, wrapping around her like a blanket in the cold, snowy street.

She had always been alone in this journey—always pushing forward, always fighting for her place. But now, for the first time, someone was telling her it was okay to feel that way, and that she had an ally, albeit in the spirit world.

"I appreciate that, Mr. Brown," Quinn said, her voice barely a whisper as she fought to keep her emotions in check.

Paul Brown's face broke into a warm smile. "Please. We're friends now, kid. Call me Paul."

For the first time in what felt like forever, Quinn smiled back, a big, genuine smile. "Okay... Paul."

And with that, the snow began to fall again, swirling around them as the dream started to fade.

Morning came, gently nudging her awake before the sun arrived, but she could somehow hear Paul's final words to her as she traveled seamlessly back to the real world: "This next chapter? It's gonna be different... for both of us. But I promise you, kid, it'll be good for you."

And already, something felt... different. She let out a breath she didn't realize she'd been holding in. The world around her felt heavier, real, pulling her back into the present. Maybe it was Nyad's youthful perspective that somehow made everything seem cleaner and clearer, though nothing about Quinn's situation was simple. Maybe it was her other world meeting with one of her childhood heroes. Or maybe... maybe she just needed to sleep on it.

Quinn took a deep breath, held it for seven seconds, and then exhaled for eight. Her fingers curled into the soft fabric of the hotel bedspread. For the first time in what felt like ages, she allowed herself to sit still, to really absorb what was happening.

She did her breathing exercise a few more times, then meditated for ten minutes before she swung her legs over the side of the bed, her feet meeting the cold hardwood floor. As she stood and stretched, she felt the weight of exhaustion lift from her body. She had been running on fumes for so long, pushing through without stopping to breathe.

She felt lighter now. And this morning came with clarity.

As Quinn exited the Four Seasons and approached the waiting black SUV, the Driver opened the rear door for her.

"Morning, Ms. Canals," the Driver greeted politely. "The ride to BWI should be a smooth one."

Quinn hesitated for a moment, looking at the open door, the path she had intended to take back to her old life. But something tugged at her.

"Actually... we're not going to BWI," she said, a quiet resolve in her voice.

She slid into the back seat, the door closing with a quiet thud, sealing her decision.

As the SUV moved smoothly through the streets of Baltimore, the familiar sights of the city rolled by the window as Quinn leaned back in her seat, lost in thought. There was so much she needed to do. But if anybody could do it, it was Quinn—known to be someone who got more done before most people were awake.

By the time Papa Canals came downstairs and walked into his kitchen that morning to microwave water for his coffee, he found himself standing in his robe, grimacing, trying to understand what he was looking at—a brand-new high-end stainless steel stove in the place of the old one which was gone.

By the time Drew had settled in at Canals' Crab Shack, working alone to prepare the place for business that day, a man in a blue work outfit was tapping on the door.

When Drew approached, he immediately noticed the nametag on the left side of the man's shirt, which read, "Lou," and the name "Lou's Appliance Repair" on the right.

"I was called here to install a pressure relief valve and some timers," Lou said, hoping it was enough to calm Drew's suspicions.

Drew exhaled, annoyed, knowing Quinn was behind this. He avoided rolling his eyes as he unlocked the door and let him in.

And by the time Gabe was walking into his classroom at the arts college, his phone was chiming to alert him of an incoming text. His arms were full— his laptop bag and coffee in one hand and a case of camera lens in the other—so he stumbled over to the desk to quickly lighten his load.

Once his hands were free, he pulled his cell from his pocket and looked at the unread message. It was from Quinn:

"OKAY. BUT UNDER ONE CONDITION... I GET A SAY ON THE FINAL CUT."

Gabe's smiling face flashed in her mind, and she could almost hear his laugh while reading her response as she looked out at Baltimore through the car window again. She felt different today—not weighed down by stress and fear, but lightened by the fuel of ambition and hunger. She hadn't felt this kind of drive in three years. Something had finally clicked into place.

ACT THREE

THE BEGINNING

As far as Traci and Pedro were concerned, their little family was set. They were both in their mid-30s at this point and earned just enough to support themselves and their six and nine-year-old kids. And then, one day out of the blue, Traci got a call from the nice lady at the Department of Human Services who helped them with their boys.

Because the Canals were known to the social worker, despite not being listed as actively looking to add to their family, she still had their number in her phonebook. So, when she connected with Traci, it was by mistake; she had actually intended to call a different "Tracy" to tell her about a child in need of foster care adoption.

Some time had passed since they'd last spoken, so the two women spent a moment catching up before the nice lady explained what she had phoned to tell the other "Tracy." It was a situation where a sweet kid had endured an incredibly rough start for someone who was not even four yet, and the lady didn't spare Traci from some of the worst stories of abuse. By this point, after having bounced around foster homes, the biological parents' rights had already been terminated, and nobody in the family wanted or was able to take the child. She told Traci that this kid just had a lifetime of "bad luck."

The fact that it was Mother's Day was not lost on Traci, but she finished the call with the lady by wishing her good luck in finding a decent family to take that kid. And then she went on with her holiday without talking to Pedro or her boys or anybody about the conversation she'd had with the nice lady. Even though she couldn't stop thinking about the kid with the bad luck, she figured she had two kids already who were doing well, and she just hadn't considered a third one—a young girl at that.

But a conversation with Drew—yes, her somewhat rebellious second child—completely changed her perspective. It happened the same Mother's Day afternoon she got the call from the nice lady. This was the third Mother's Day Drew had spent with Traci, and after handing her the predictable card and flowers, he told her that he'd had five different mothers and that she was the best one he's ever had and the only one he's ever given a card and flowers to. He surprisingly went on and on expressing his feelings of love for her and how "lucky" he felt now that she was his mother.

There was something about the word "luck" that Traci never liked. In fun, meaningless situations, sure, let's call something "luck" or someone "lucky." But in real life, she just couldn't bring herself to believe that stuff happened by chance. She felt things, whether good or bad, were meant to happen—whether we know, or will ever know, the meaning.

Drew was never the most verbal child when it came to affection, but that day opened up something in him, and in turn, he opened up something in his mother. "Lucky to have her" was okay for a boy to say, but Traci felt like their connection was far more design than chance, and that she was as blessed to have him as he obviously felt to have her. They were meant to have each other.

So this made her think about the random phone call she'd gotten earlier from the nice lady about the little girl with "bad luck." And she couldn't help but wonder: was it really the wrong number the woman had called, or was it the right number at the wrong time?

The very next morning, Traci called the lady back and asked if she could meet the kid that day, and the lady agreed, even adding that she never did get in touch with the "Tracy" she'd intended to reach the day before.

* * *

The warm, sleek, glassy interior of Starlings HQ buzzed with an anxious energy as Greta McFly paced around the small conference room. Her mind was clearly racing as she shuffled through papers, scanning every detail like someone searching for a last-minute miracle.

Two team staff members—Lee, a nerdy, androgynous woman in her mid-20s, and Hazel, a punk-rocker type in her mid-30s—sat at the table, equally tense. The team had been in crisis mode for 24 hours now, and with the season drawing nearer, they were running out of time and options.

"No, Johnson just isn't a good fit..." Greta muttered, more to herself than anyone else, before abruptly raising her head.

"Mara and Thompson both took jobs with other franchises, so we can scratch them," Lee chimed in, her voice calm but clipped.

"I still think Johnson could do it if we gave him an assistant and another coordinator," Hazel interjected, trying to sound hopeful.

Greta stopped, her eyes narrowing with frustration. "Fuck! We don't have the budget for two additional hires. Plus, Johnson is asking for more than we allotted for Canals, which was already 20% more than we had to spend in the first place—"

Suddenly, a knock at the open door broke the tension in the room. The three of them turned their heads in unison to see Quinn standing in the doorway.

Greta blinked in surprise. "Quinn?" she said, still processing the fact that Quinn was in Baltimore, and not on a flight out.

The hallway outside of the conference room felt warmer than before as Quinn walked beside Greta, her footsteps slow and measured. Greta, ever the straight-to-the-point GM, couldn't help but glance sideways at Quinn, trying to read the situation.

"Your flight left an hour ago," Greta remarked, her tone neutral, but her curiosity unmistakable. "Should I be reading anything into the fact that you're here and not on it?"

Quinn took her time before responding— thoughts were clear now. She exhaled deeply, as if releasing the last bit of weight she'd been carrying for days. "I always liked the idea of having a north star—a goal that sets the path for the direction I want to go," she began, her voice steady but thoughtful.

Greta slowed her pace, listening carefully.

"Everything I've done to this point, all the hobbies I practice, all the books I read for leisure— there are no accidents. No coincidences. No mistakes," Quinn continued, her gaze forward as they walked. "It all matters. It all contributes. It all builds toward my ultimate goal: my north star."

They stopped walking, standing still for a moment in the quiet hallway.

Quinn turned to face Greta, her expression

resolute. "I want to do special things. I believe football—coaching—will help me do those things." She took a deep breath, her final decision settling in. "So... I've changed my mind. I want to be here if... if you'll still have me."

Greta's eyes widened, and a smile slowly spread across her face, broad and genuine. For a moment, it looked like she was trying to restrain herself, to stay professional. But it was no use—she was ecstatic.

"I want to hug you. Can I hug you? No," Greta quickly backtracked, shaking her head. "I won't hug you. It's illegal. And it's creepy."

Quinn smiled, her own tension easing as she extended her hand. Greta shook it enthusiastically, almost bouncing on her heels.

"So, ah... wanna meet your team?" Greta asked, barely able to contain her excitement.

Outside of the building in the rear was also an entire state-of-the-art practice field that you couldn't possibly guess was there if you only saw the building from the front. In fact, there was a lot about the building that was unassuming.

So it was no surprise that the rookie carrier didn't exactly know where to go, even after reading the instructions on the box that said: "Enter through the west side lower rear electric door."

She sighed as she closed the back of the truck and read the directions again as she made her way toward the building.

Alana Ari had the kind of presence that made people stop and take notice. At 25, she was average height, but her lean, sculpted body from years of intense training on the track made her appear taller in person than on TV. Her olive skin had a natural glow; her face, sharp and striking, reflected her focus—high cheekbones and almond-shaped eyes that had a way of cutting through any distraction when she was locked in.

Her heritage was as important to her as her athletic achievements. Raised with a strong sense of identity and community, she balanced her cultural traditions with the demanding life of an elite athlete. She wore a small Magen David pendant around her neck, a subtle but constant reminder of who she was and the values she carried with her.

In the world of track and field—sprinting to be precise—she was a name people knew around these parts, a name they expected to see in the headlines. She had been the pride of Maryland for years—the surprising local track star who was supposed to make it all the way to the Olympics. Her parents wanted her to be the first Jewish-American woman to win gold in the 100 and 200 meter events. And she actually had the time in practice, but her promising career had hit a wall when it counted. Despite getting to two Olympic games and being a favorite to reach the finals, something had gone wrong. She just... wasn't fast enough, not that day. The failure was public, the disappointment palpable.

Yet, despite her losses, Alana carried herself with no need for external validation. She wasn't one to sulk or crumble under the weight of expectations. She still had that determination in her eyes, even if the Olympic dream had slipped through her fingers. There was a resilience to her—a refusal to be defined by that one failure. Alana was driven, not just by the success she'd had in the past, but by the need to prove that one setback didn't determine her worth.

Off the track, Alana was reserved, often introspective. She wasn't the type to be the life of the party, but her presence was always felt in a room. She'd had to recalibrate her life since failing to accomplish her goal, finding new ways to channel her energy. Her transition into the public sphere wasn't as glamorous as her Olympic dreams. Instead of endorsements and podium finishes, she had taken up a role as a delivery driver—an odd, almost jarring contrast for someone who had once been one of the fastest women in the country.

But even in that, there was a sense of purpose. She didn't see the job as beneath her; it was a means to an end, another step in her journey, however unexpected. And besides, AriQuick Parcel Service was her mother's company—the fastest-growing same-day courier start-up in the country. So sure, Alana could've chosen a cushy front office position, a chance to be groomed to run the whole operation someday, but she deliberately chose field work—something she knew she'd never get comfortable doing. That way, she could use the time to figure out her next ideal step.

Her loosely coiled hair—pulled back into a neat ponytail today—bounced as she hustled toward the west side of the building.

She looked around for the door that was supposed to be there, an electric door to be exact, but didn't see anything resembling a door. She did, however, see a tall, black metal gate, so she ventured through, hoping to find this mysterious door somewhere on the other side.

Instead, she stumbled upon an incredible scene, where hundreds of people—women of all shapes, sizes, and colors—were engaged in all kinds of cardio and calisthenics and endurance drills that all seemed to centered around throwing and catching footballs.

What is this place? she wondered. And as if the question was being answered right then and there, her eyes drifted over to a banner of an NFFL logo: National Flag Football League - Women's Division.

On the opposite side and opposite end of the 70 yards of finely manicured grass, Quinn stood at the edge of the field next to Greta. The weight of her decision settled firmly on her shoulders. The expansive space stretched out in front of her, alive with movement and energy.

Quinn scanned the field, watching the

organized chaos unfold, her eyes lingering on the athletes pushing themselves through the drills, forcing their bodies to the limit for this audition. The sheer number of these women was impressive, but also overwhelming. Somewhere in this crowd was her team—her responsibility now.

Greta stood beside her, watching her closely, a smirk tugging at her lips. She couldn't contain her excitement.

Quinn, however, showed zero emotion one way or the other. Her concentration was impossible to read. "So... where's... who is the team?" she asked, her voice steady but edged with the uncertainty of the moment.

"Well," Greta said, handing her a folder thick with bound papers, "There are 105 women here. 15 of them will make it. It's *your* job... to decide which 15 that'll be."

Quinn opened the folder, glancing at the pages filled with headshots and notes on each athlete. Her eyes flicked back to the field as she took a deep breath, feeling the enormity of the task in front of her. It wasn't just about picking a team. This was the start of something new, something uncharted.

Meanwhile, as Alana, who was still holding the package she was there to deliver, stood by watching the workout, she hadn't noticed that the black gate behind her didn't close after she came through it.

So that meant Swifty, the cute, blonde pit bull

who had escaped the animal rescue guy the day before, could easily shimy her way through. She, too, was curious about what was going on on the field.

Alana's eyes were fixed on the six women lined up at the end zone right there where she stood, ready to race—the 40-yard dash. A trainer stood off to the side, holding up a starter pistol. The women braced themselves, eyes focused ahead.

POW!

The gun fired into the air, and the women took off running. But the sound startled Swifty, sending the dog charging toward the field… and right toward Alana, still holding the package she hadn't delivered.

The dog charging toward her scared her, and in a split second, she dropped the box and bolted!

With Swifty in hot pursuit, Alana dashed onto the field, her legs moving with impossible speed. Despite starting well behind the other women, she quickly gained on them, her athleticism on full display. Even Swifty, despite the name, couldn't keep up with her.

Alana zipped past the other runners effortlessly, her body moving with the grace and power of someone who had spent years perfecting the art of speed.

The trainer, stopwatch in hand, stared in disbelief as Alana flew by. Her eyes darted from the clock to Quinn and Greta, her mouth hanging open in shock.

The stopwatch read 4.9 seconds! And that was

starting from behind everyone else and well after them.

"Who is that?" Quinn asked, her gaze following Alana as she continued running around the field, Swifty still chasing after her.

Greta didn't respond. She didn't need to. The two women exchanged a look, both of them thinking the same thing. They had just witnessed something extraordinary.

As Alana continued to outrun the dog, easily weaving between and around the athletes as they laughed, Quinn felt the familiar spark of excitement—the electrifying feeling, knowing that life had thrown her new challenge… in the form of flag.

With crossed arms and a piercing stare, she once again gave the field her undivided attention. This? This was just the beginning.

END OF EPISODE ONE

DEDICATED TO
KAMALA HARRIS

ABOUT THE AUTHOR

Kayona is a 2x Emmy Award-winning filmmaker best known for her work with sport-centered and female-driven stories. Hailing from our nation's capital, Kayona started her career in entertainment as a radio DJ; her entrepreneurial spirit led her down a storied path that included her dream of telling stories for screens and inspired her award-winning multimedia project, OF MUSIC AND MEN.

In her role as a writer/director, music videos and short films have brought awards recognition and strengthened her artistic fingerprint as a visionary, as she continues to impact and influence even greater audiences. Continuing to amplify her unique perspective, Kayona lends her talents to bolster sports stories on the world's biggest stages, including the Super Bowl and the NCAA Basketball Championship.

Kayona is the winner of various fellowships and grants from Roadmap Writers (screenwriting) to the Commission on Arts and Humanities for literature and media. In addition to her roles as a speaker and voice artist, Kayona is also the founder of the entertainment venture, Siingle, a 2024 Black Ambition mentee, a program co-founded by Pharrell Williams for rising entrepreneurs.